RETRIBUTION

SILENT COVE BOOK TWO

ANNE L. PARKS

FIRESIDE PUBLISHING, LLC

Silent Cove: Retribution
Copyright 2017 Fireside Publishing, LLC

All rights reserved. Except as permitted under the U.S. Copyright Act of 1976, no part of this publication may be reproduced, distributed, or transmitted in any form or by any means, or stored in a database or retrieval system, without the prior written permission of the author.

This book is a work of fiction.

Names of characters, places, and events are the construction of the author, except those locations that are well-known and of general knowledge, and all are used fictitiously. Any resemblance to persons living or dead is coincidental, and great care was taken to design places, locations, or businesses that fit into the regional landscape without actual identification; as such, resemblance to actual places, locations, or businesses is coincidental. Any mention of a branded item, artistic work, or well-known business establishment, is used for authenticity in the work of fiction and was chosen by the author because of personal preference, its high quality, or the authenticity it lends to the work of fiction; the author has received no remuneration, either monetary or in-kind, for use of said product names, artistic work, or business establishments, and mention is not intended as advertising, nor does it constitute an endorsement. The author is solely responsible for content. Material from this work in Silent Cove: Awakening by Deanndra Hall and/or Silent Cove: Banishing by Jax Jillian is used with the author's permission.

Cover design and formatting, Buoni Amici Press, LLC

Editing, M.J. Price

Proofing, Emmy Hamilton

Disclaimer:

Material in this work of fiction is of a graphic nature and not intended for audiences under 18 years of age.

ACKNOWLEDGMENTS

Everything is better when you do it with friends…and this has been more fun than I could have imagined. Thanks to Deanndra Hall for asking me to be a part of this trilogy. I loved the idea when you first told me about it, and enjoyed every minute spent writing about a haunted inn with a creepy little boy. With the addition of Jax Jillian, we have put together the best ghost stories ever told…yeah, I may be biased, but working with both of you has been a true labor of love.

Nothing would have been written without my awesome sprinting partners Melinda, Selena, Toni, Jill, and Kendra. Thanks to my editor, MJ Price, who always has the best suggestions and comments while respecting my voice. I wouldn't be half the author I am without the help, guidance, and swift kick in the ass from Drue Hoffman of Buoni Amici Press. She is also the mastermind behind all three covers for Silent Cove. Debra Presley, also from Buoni Amici Press, put together an amazing trailer. They are the best team any author can have behind them.

Of course, I am always very appreciative of readers who will take a risk to read a book, and become immersed in the words and worlds we weave for your enjoyment. It is truly a joy and an honor to publish books that you enjoy

PROLOGUE

1923

"You simply must help me, Vi."

Viola paced back and forth in front of her sister, worrying her bottom lip with her teeth.

Of course. Eliza has a problem and now it becomes my burden. Some things never change.

Eliza leaned over the long butcher block table that separated the two women. "If Maurice finds out I'm—" her gaze darted around the room, "—pregnant." The whispered word lingered in the air between them.

Viola wrapped her arms across her chest and took a calming breath. Dealing with Eliza was exasperating on a good day. At the moment, Viola's blood pressure was through the roof. "Well, maybe you should've thought of that before you got into bed with a married man."

"Don't you dare get sanctimonious with me, Viola," Eliza sneered. "You have a job, and a nice house to live in where you can raise your daughter—all because I bed a married man. Don't pretend that I'm the only one reaping the benefits of my relationship with Maurice."

Knowing Eliza was right did nothing to quell the fury blazing a fiery path through Viola's veins. She wanted to believe that she would've been able to get a job working for Maurice and Delilah Cambridge without relying on her sister's adulterous affair. Viola knew what the townsfolk of Chistine were saying about her, noticed how they would avoid her at the grocery store, how they would speak to her at church only after she had spoken to them first.

Being associated with Eliza, the town whore, had nearly damaged Viola's reputation beyond repair. People could be cruel in their Christian values, and often found guilt through association with those they perceived as less than godly individuals.

What did Viola care? Those were the same people who would come to parties at the mansion Maurice had spent millions to build and then given to his mistress. They were all two-faced Saturday night sinners who would beg for forgiveness in church on Sunday morning. They were no better than Maurice and Eliza.

Certainly no better than Viola, who was doing her damnedest to provide for her young daughter, Marjorie. Viola hadn't planned to be a young widow. The life of a fisherman is not his—it belongs to the sea gods and they decide when it's time to call a man home. Viola knew this when she married Harold, but had hoped the inevitable wouldn't have been so early in their marriage.

Now, standing in the kitchen, a servant to her younger sister, Viola considered where she had been a year ago. No way of paying the mortgage, zero money for food, and no one else in town hiring a woman whose only experience had been cooking and cleaning all her life. It was a godsend that Maurice had taken his young mistresses advice and hired Viola, provided a room in the servant's quarters for her and Marjorie, and paid good wages.

Viola took another deep breath, her resolve to make her sister pay the piper and reap the consequences of her actions quickly dissolved. Marjorie did not deserve to have to grow up without a roof over her head, food in her mouth, or the carefree existence children are entitled to have in their youth. Getting fired for insubordination was not a good plan, and Viola was certain Maurice would do whatever Eliza requested—even letting go of a cook that made "the best meals he'd ever eaten". Maurice was far too smitten with Eliza and her many talents in the bedroom to give a spit about Viola and her predicament.

Viola sighed, her shoulders dropped from the expectation that made the air in the room heavy. "What do you want me to do?"

Eliza squealed as if she was a little girl, ran around the table, and hugged Viola's neck. "I knew I could count on you to save me."

Another vestige of Viola's dignity cracked and shattered in the depths of her soul.

What have I gotten myself into...

1

Lansing dropped her bag next to the reception desk and rang the bell. The Silent Cove Bed and Breakfast was quaint and looked exactly like the pictures on the website. That had to be a first. So many times she'd arrived at a converted early American home to find the website photos were heavily edited and provided a more glamorous view of the place than the reality.

"Good afternoon," a young woman said. "You must be Ms. Abbott? Welcome to Silent Cove Bed and Breakfast. I'm Carmen." Lansing smiled at the petite woman with long brunette hair. She had a sweet smile that lit up her brown eyes. "I see you'll be with us for a couple of weeks, is that correct?"

"Yes, but I may need to extend my reservation," Lansing said. "I'm doing some research in the area and not sure exactly how long it will take to get what I need. Unfortunately, I may not know until right before my current reservation is up whether or not I'll be staying longer. Will that be a problem?"

"Hmm..." Carmen clicked a few keys on the computer keyboard. Her eyebrows furrowed for a moment as she stared intently at the computer screen. "I don't think so…" she drew out. "I don't have anyone who has made a reservation and specifically requested your room." She looked up at Lansing and smiled. "At any rate, if someone does, we can always move you to another room, if that's okay?"

"Absolutely." Lansing pulled her wallet from her purse and fished out her credit card. "That actually might be preferable—it will give me a chance to experience the inn from a different vantage point. And if you'd like, feel free to add a deposit for another two week period, just in case I do need to stay."

Carmen shook her head. "That won't be necessary. We're happy to accommodate you, and hope you enjoy your stay with us, no matter what the length." She took the credit card Lansing extended to her and swiped it through the machine. "You said you're here to do some research?"

"Yes, I'm on sabbatical from Plymouth University in Rhode Island. I teach early American history and I'm researching for a new book about this region of the country."

"Sounds interesting, and Chistine has a great deal of fascinating history—if you can get the locals to open up about it." Carmen leaned in closer. "Bit closed mouthed about some of their more colorful history, if you know what I mean?"

Lansing laughed in agreement. She was all too familiar with how secretive people could be about some of the darker realities of the past, preferring to maintain the more socially acceptable versions of history. "So, I take it you know some of the colorful aspects of the area?"

"Some, but I'm not from around here. My husband, Angelo, and I moved out here from California, and ended up buying this place. There's probably enough history on this piece of property to write an encyclopedia, but we had a very difficult time getting any of the locals to talk to us about it."

"Really? What kind of history?"

"Well, I assume you saw the disclaimer on the website about some of the paranormal activity we experience routinely, and if you read any of the reviews, you know many visitors have encountered some of our long-term occupants—"

"Yes, I did see those, but honestly—no disrespect intended—I figured it was all a marketing ploy."

Carmen chuckled. "We have taken what we have and decided to make it work for us, that much is true. But I can assure you the claims are real. It took some doing, but we've finally come to an *agreement* with our ethereal guests so we can all live harmoniously. For the most part, anyway—ghosts can be quirky." Carmen handed Lansing an envelope. "You're in the red room on the second floor, with a view of the gardens. We serve breakfast and dinner, but if you need lunch, we're happy to whip something up for you. Just let us know. Mealtimes are listed on the information sheet in your room. Feel free to wander the grounds at your leisure. If you do walk the grounds, wear the amulet in the box on the desk in your room. Any questions?"

Lansing shook her head, certain she had a thousand questions, but not sure what they were at that moment. A lot of information had just been provided, and she was still stuck on having to wear an amulet to walk the grounds. Was it all a ruse to keep up the haunted inn marketing scheme?

Carmen stepped around to the front of the reception desk. "I'll take your bag and escort you upstairs."

Gently pushing the door open to Lansing's room,

Carmen placed the bag on the luggage rack and handed her the key. "If you need anything, let me know. Otherwise, all the activities are listed on the sheet on the desk." She pointed to a small writing desk, then quietly slipped out of the room, closing the door behind her.

Lansing looked around the room. Carmen had done an excellent job updating the inn while retaining the essence of the Victorian time period through the furnishings and decor. The damask wallpaper was a rich red with gold flowers and matched the bedding. The chairs and window treatments were red and gold stripes. Lansing felt as if she had stepped back in time. It was the perfect setting to get into the mindset of the early settlers in the area. Although, not many people that resided in the small fishing town had lived quite this extravagantly on a fisherman's pay.

Now, where to start?

The legends of the sea had always been great fodder for myths of gods and ghosts. Most academics and historians believed ghost stories were a bi-product of a lack of scientific knowledge and were a way to understand the unexplained. Things modern humans take for granted as fact were potentially in a hypothetical state of experimentation, or nowhere near discovery, when the country was in its infancy. Lansing strived to separate the fact from fiction, the myths from reality. Tall tales from truth. The paranormal from the tangible.

But what if there was no distinction between otherworldly entities and substantive existence? What if ghosts were as real as living, breathing humans? The internal struggle to accept what could not be proven was one of the main reasons Lansing had decided to delve into a subject most academics shunned. There had to be some truth behind the stories passed down through generations of families. Wasn't it a little arrogant to believe the living were the only inhabitants of the earth?

Lansing had no answers, but many questions, and what she hoped was an open mind. She wanted to know the truth, but did she possess the ability to believe what she might see because it was easier to explain it away as a product of her imagination?

She glanced out the window facing the gardens at the back of the house. "That's as good a place as any to start looking." Picking up the amulet Carmen had mentioned, Lansing left her room and descended the stairs in search of the inn's ghostly inhabitants.

THE VARIOUS GARDEN paths led to the edge of a forest. A trail meandered into the woods at the back of the property. Lansing followed the signs pointing to the cottage. The information packet provided at check-in told of the graves at the cottage and the events of the New Year's Eve party in 1925 that ended in the deaths of three people. She sat on the bench, hoping to see the infamous William, who was neither fully dead nor fully living, but somehow existed in limbo. According to the notes, William would remain that way until his daughter, Delilah, accepted her death and crossed over. At that time, William would be released from the property, and—*what?*—be able to die? That was still a mystery, but the options were quite intriguing to consider.

After wandering around the cottage grounds for nearly an hour, Lansing decided to seek out William another time, and headed back to the main house. The foliage of the trees created a canopy over the trail. Sunlight filtered through in streams, providing enough light to see the trail, but cooling the air significantly. The sun had baked Lansing at the cottage and she welcomed the cool air that wrapped around her. She breathed in the earthy smell of the forest floor mixed with the hint of evergreens, maples, and oaks. The tree trunks were huge, suggesting they were there before the first settlers came upon the land. She thought of William, and hoped that if Delilah ever finally rested in peace, William would become one of these majestic trees. Still a part of the land, still living, but no longer human. Seemed like a nice fate for a man who had spent so many years stuck in such an odd existence.

Around a bend, Lansing saw a woman standing next to a large oak. In her hand was a tissue that covered her mouth. As Lansing approached, she could hear faint whimpering come from the woman and considered not intruding on her private grief.

A branch cracked under Lansing's foot. The woman's head jerked up, her hollow gaze encased Lansing in ice, and paralyzed her where she stood. Something about the woman didn't seem—*real*. She had an aura about her, a mist shrouding her, making her seem *transparent*.

Lansing blinked a few times, but the woman was gone. Turning in a circle, Lansing searched for any sight of the mysterious woman. It was as if she had disappeared into thin air.

Could that have been one of the ghosts?

Lansing chuckled at the thought. It hadn't taken long for her to get swept up in the haunted mansion hype being peddled by the inn. Whether or not the woman was a spirit was one thing. What she was doing there was the real question.

The tree didn't seem any different than others in the forest. So what had made the woman cry?

Lansing stepped closer. A large rock sat at the base of the trunk, partially buried. Along the bottom of the rock, nearly hidden by the fallen dead leaves, was a crudely carved inscription. Lansing pushed the debris aside and brushed the dirt from the stone.

1935

Lansing gasped.

Was this a tombstone? Who lay beneath the tree, and why weren't they in the graveyard at the cottage?

Lansing wandered back to the inn, her mind mulling over the possibilities of whose grave she had stumbled upon. Was it perhaps a beloved pet? That was an option, she guessed. Lansing had buried many pets in her family's backyard growing up.

And then there was the woman. Why would anyone be crying over an animal that died in 1935?

Too many questions, and only one way she could think of to get the answers. She entered the kitchen through the side door. Carmen was speaking with an elderly woman as they shucked corn.

"I apologize for interrupting," Lansing said.

"Not at all," Carmen responded. "This is our fabulous cook, Marjorie. Her family has been working on the property since it was built."

Marjorie nodded with a smile at Lansing, but went back to cleaning the ears of corn. Lansing studied the woman, not completely sure she wasn't among the dearly departed. The woman had to be nearly a hundred years old.

"What can we do for you, Ms. Abbott?" Carmen asked, wiping her hands on a towel.

"Please, call me Lansing." Lansing struggled with how to approach the two women with her questions. It was one thing to discuss ghosts and graves in the abstract, quite another to ask about them as if they were an everyday acquaintance.

Best, perhaps, to ease into the conversation…

"While I was walking the trail from the cottage, I came upon what I believe is a small grave…under a tree…do you know anything about it?"

Carmen gently shook her head from side to side. "I've seen it—the one right after you come around the bend—but I have no idea who it belongs to…if it *is* an actual grave." Carmen grabbed an ear of corn and pulled back the layers sheathing the kernels. "To tell you the truth, with all the other strange things that go on around here, I sort of put the grave out of my mind." She glanced over at Marjorie. "Do you know whose grave that could be?"

"No. I've asked William about it—" she took a tentative glance at Lansing, most likely to see her reaction to admitting to having conversations with a pseudo-ethereal presence—"but he would just brush the question aside as if it was nothing. I guess after a while I just got used to it being a mystery and never gave it much mind. It just *is*…never seemed important as to who was there."

Carmen glanced at Marjorie, then at Lansing, and quirked up an eyebrow. *What the hell?* A grave is on the property and no one knows what, if anything, lies beneath? *I guess with the overabundance of paranormal activity on the grounds, one tiny grave under a tree isn't a big deal.*

Lansing lifted a few strands of corn silk and ran them through her fingers. "There was a woman standing by the tree when I first came upon it. She didn't say anything to me, but it looked as if she was crying. As soon as she saw me, she disappeared."

"Disappeared?" Carmen asked.

"Yes. One minute she was there and then—" Lansing waved her hand in the air. "Gone."

"What was she wearing?" Marjorie asked without looking up.

"A pale yellow dress, beaded, fell just below her knees," Lansing said. "And I think there was fringe along the bottom."

Carmen and Marjorie looked at each other, slow smiles spreading across their faces. "Eliza," they said in unison.

"The mistress who died?"

"Yep," Carmen answered with a chuckle. "Congratulations, you met your first ghost."

Lansing stared at the two women for a moment. Somehow they felt discovering the ghost of a woman who had died almost a hundred years earlier, standing over an unmarked grave in the woods, was quite an accomplishment. Lansing was still struggling with whether or not she believed she had just seen a spirit.

"Usually our ethereal guest don't interact with people while they're wearing the amulets," Carmen said, pointing to the pin Lansing was wearing.

"Well, I wouldn't really call our meeting an interaction. As soon as she saw me, she left. Do you mind if I do some investigating into who—or what—is buried there? I promise not to bother any of the other guests."

Carmen grabbed a large pot from the rack above her head. "As long as you don't start digging it up, I have no problem."

The thought hadn't crossed Lansing's mind, but now she couldn't stop thinking about it. What would be the harm in just seeing if there was actually anything under there?

Marjorie narrowed one eye as she cast her gaze toward Lansing. "We like to live in harmony with our dearly departed friends. Digging up graves is not something that will promote good will."

Lansing couldn't argue with that. Besides, she really wasn't keen on uncovering someone's skull. "Well, thanks so much for the information."

The two women smiled and went back to work. Lansing mindlessly walked down the hall until she was on the front porch. Rocking chairs lined the veranda, and she sat down and peered out over the front gardens. This was what she had wanted—to learn more about the north east and it's many stories—and to separate fact from fiction. History from folklore. To determine if people who lived centuries ago were indeed still connected to the land, unable to move on and accept death peacefully.

She had wanted this...but did she believe it was really, truly happening?

2

An email sat in Tucker Kingsley's inbox from his father. He smiled at the litany of poorly taken pictures of the various places Tucker's parents were visiting on their around-the-world cruise. After years of working nights and weekends to make more money than was needed, Tucker's father, Robert, had finally retired. The cruise was his mother's reward for sticking it out all those years, essentially raising Tucker on her own.

Despite rarely seeing his father, Tucker had a close relationship with the man. To his credit, when Robert was around, he was all in—playing catch with Tucker, taking his wife, Marne, out for romantic dinners, and being one hundred percent engaged with his family. The times were brief, but packed with memories. Yeah, Tucker would've liked more time with his father, but he had seen many of his friends whose dads were around day after day and didn't spend half as much time with their kids.

And it wasn't as if Tucker had grown up wanting for anything. They lived in a nice house in Boston.

Tucker had riding lessons, tennis coaches, attended baseball camp every summer, and had a shiny new car on his sixteenth birthday. Life was not a hardship growing up. He learned to appreciate what he did have, and not dwell on what he didn't.

His mother had made sure he saw how different life was for less fortunate people, and insisted he understand a man was measured by his acts and deeds and not his words or the balance of his bank account. Tucker spent time working in soup kitchens, handing out coats and shoes to homeless people in the winter, and delivering meals to the elderly. But Marne Kingsley was not satisfied with just the perfunctory acts, she wanted Tucker to really understand that being poor, or homeless, or without the luxury of eating a home cooked meal, or sleeping in a warm, dry bed could happen to anyone. So she made sure he visited with all those he served soup to, or gave a coat, because she wanted him to see them as people—as equals—and not someone lesser than himself.

It was the best gift she could've ever given him, and molded him into the man he had become.

Tucker chuckled at the picture of his mother standing next to a seawall somewhere in the south of France, one hand on her head to keep her hat from blowing away. She was laughing. Tucker's heart surged with happiness. She deserved to have fun and act like a kid again.

His desk phone rang. "Tucker Kingsley."

"Mr. Kingsley, my name is Duncan Shakely. I'm a lawyer in Chistine, Maine. Are you, perhaps, related to Robert Kingsley?"

Tucker sat up in his chair. "Yes, he's my father."

"I wonder if you wouldn't mind giving me his number? It's imperative I get in touch with him."

"I'm sorry, but my father is out of the country and not due to return for six months. Is there something I can help you with?"

There was a brief pause before the man spoke again. "Yes, I suppose you would be the next of kin, if your father's not available."

Tucker grabbed a notepad from his drawer, and tried to recall why the name Chistine sounded familiar to him.

"I'm sorry to inform you over the phone, but your uncle, Walter Kingsley, has passed away. As you and your father seem to be his only surviving relatives, I was wondering about what arrangements were to be made for him."

Of course. Tucker remembered trips from his youth to visit his Uncle Walter and his father's sister, Cora, in Chistine. It had been many years since they'd been back to his father's hometown.

"Your uncle had a very sizable estate," Shakely said, pulling Tucker from his memories. "Would you be able to come to Chistine to settle his affairs?"

Tucker quickly pulled his calendar up on his computer screen. Only one meeting was problematic that week, the rest could be rescheduled. "Yes, I can come down. You say he has a large estate…can you give me some idea what that entails?"

"Well, large in the sense that he had collected many things over the years. Really the only thing of value is the house, which for the area, is somewhat substantial."

"So—really—it'll just be a matter of clearing it out and putting it on the market?"

Duncan chuckled. "Unfortunately, your uncle was a bit of a hoarder. Cleaning it out will not be a simple task."

Wonderful…just what I wanted to hear.

"I'll need to clear a few things from my schedule, but I should be there by tomorrow sometime. Can you recommend somewhere to stay?"

"The nicest place in town is Silent Cove Bed and Breakfast."

3

The gardens at Silent Cove were mesmerizing, and more importantly, relaxing. Lansing grabbed a romance from the shelf in the library—a secret guilty pleasure she was rarely able to enjoy—and sat on the grass under a large oak tree. She had only intended to read for an hour, but the cool breeze and sweet, flowery scents lulled her into a world of mystery, suspense, and hot sex for over two hours.

Sex...

When was the last time she'd had sex?

The fact she couldn't remember was a pretty good indication it'd been a while. The last guy she had dated was an English professor at the university. The discussions between them had been stimulating at the start of their relationship, but the brooding personality that first attracted her had worn on her over time, and she was tired of the man's inability to find pleasure in anything. Even sex had to be discussed as if it had some deep, dark meaning that defined them as heathens. It was one thing to over analyze life and literature, but Lansing just wanted to enjoy having her mind and body rocked by a scream-inducing orgasm.

When it looked as if she wasn't going to get anything she desired from being with Brent, she'd told him the relationship was over. In typical fashion, he wanted to meet with her one last time to discuss what had gone wrong. Lansing knew that would only lead to a long-winded discussion that would take hours from her that she would never get back. Not long after the break-up, Lansing decided to take a sabbatical.

Closing her book, Lansing headed back into the kitchen to see if she could get a drink. Marjorie was alone snapping green beans into a large bowl. She looked up as Lansing stepped inside the room.

"Can I help you, Miss?"

"I'm sorry to bother you, but could I get a glass of lemonade?" Lansing asked, holding the book behind her. Why was she worried about Marjorie seeing what she was reading? Because the woman might think less of Lansing? Who the hell cares?

Lansing, apparently. She was old enough to have been brought up under the stigma of reading romance, and remembered her mother secreting her "naughty" books when her father would enter the room.

Marjorie handed a glass to Lansing and returned to her work. Lansing sipped the slightly sweet, slightly tart beverage, welcoming the coolness as it slid down her throat. Sitting on a stool across the work table from Marjorie, she picked up a green bean, snapped off the ends, and deposited it into the bowl.

"I haven't done this since I was a kid," Lansing said before Marjorie could object to the help. "My mother and grandmother would spend hours snapping green beans and then another day canning them. I would help, sometimes—when it was too hot outside to play, or my brothers refused to let me join in their fun. My mother and grandmother would talk endlessly about family members I had never met." Lansing shook her head at the memory. She smiled, a flood of warmth washed over her as she recalled her grandmother.

"I spent many a day in this very kitchen doing the same thing with my mother," Marjorie said. "Some of my best memories are standing right in this very spot, talking and laughing—" she let out a heavy sigh, but a smile played across her lips.

"You grew up here?" Lansing tossed a handful of snapped beans into the bowl.

"Oh, yes…I barely recall a time I didn't live here. I was very young when we moved onto the estate."

"Where did you live before you came here?"

"In a house in town—my mother would point it out when we would go by it on our way to church—lived there until my daddy died."

"You must've lost him at a young age," Lansing commented.

"Yes, I was only two or three years old." Marjorie slowed her work, a hollowness shrouded her gaze. "He was a fisherman. Worked for William, as a matter of fact. I think I remember when they told Mother he was gone. She cried and cried for days." She blinked a few times, and focused on the beans once more. "May not be an actual memory, just something I conjured up from the story being told time and again."

"How did he die, if you don't mind me asking?"

"Oh, no—of course not. They were on the water when a big storm came through. It's very dangerous on a ship when there is a storm. They had a greenhorn on deck—got caught up in some line—Daddy went out to untangle him, and was washed overboard."

"That's so sad," Lansing said.

"It was," Marjorie exhaled. "I barely remember him, except from pictures. Anyway, without my daddy's income, Mother couldn't afford the house. She got the job out here, and we moved in right after it was built."

"So, you've probably seen more than your share of strange things over the years?"

Marjorie snorted. "You could say that. After a while, I just got so accustomed to the peculiarities they no longer affected me." She chuckled. "It wasn't always that way, though. I remember telling Mother I would see people, but she never believed me."

"You mean Eliza, Maurice, and Delilah? Or William?" Lansing asked. Marjorie glanced at her with a quizzical brow. "I read about the history on the website."

"Well, yes, I saw them often because they would come to the house—especially Delilah, and of course, William. Delilah was always a nasty one. So bitter at the end of her life, she seems to have dragged it with her into death. I feel sorry for her. She killed my aunt Eliza and Maurice out of jealousy. I always assumed she had killed herself to escape the repercussions, but also to alleviate the sadness. Obviously didn't work. Her spirit is so volatile."

"I guess I never thought about how a person enters death, and that being how they exist in the after life."

"I don't think that's how it is for most people. I think those that cross over—go into the light, as it were—are probably pretty content. But Delilah *refuses* to let go of any of it. While she is here, she prevents Eliza and William from crossing over. I haven't seen Maurice, so maybe he left both women behind," she tittered. "That would be just like Maurice to do what he wants and the rest be damned."

"Do you think Delilah is the reason Eliza is still here?"

Marjorie shrugged. "I don't claim to be an expert in the after life, but I don't know of any other reason she would remain."

"Do you think your mother knew about the ghosts and dismissed them to protect you?"

"Oh, yes. For many years after William's death, I still believed him to be alive. I remember when I found out—his wife, Zora Sue had brought her kids out to play on the grounds, and I asked why they didn't just come out when William came to work. Zora looked at me like I had gone crazy. Mother was mortified and tried to laugh it off. Later she told me William was a unique person, but that Zora believed he was dead, and that was how William preferred it. I never spoke of him again."

Lansing thought Silent Cove would've been the perfect place to grow up, playing in the gardens, and exploring the forest. But it must have been confusing and a bit freakish for a young child. "Since his death, William has lived in the cottage?"

"Well, yes," Marjorie lifted one shoulder in a half shrug. "I always wondered what happened to the woman and the little boy that lived there before William took up residency."

That caught Lansing's attention. "There were previous tenants?"

"I always thought so. When I was growing up, I would see a woman and a little boy, but Mother said I was foolish, and conjuring things in my head. Told me to stop wasting time on such things. After a while, I stopped talking about them, too."

"Did you ever ask William about them?"

"Yes, but he denied it. I guess maybe I did imagine the whole thing."

Lansing wondered if that was true. Although, with the sordid past associated with the property, perhaps there were other ghosts no one knew about. "This house has such a tragic past."

"Yes, there have been more than enough deaths associated with this place." Marjorie snapped the last beans, tossed them into the bowl, and let out a satisfying sigh.

Carmen came into the kitchen, her arms loaded with bags. "Wow, I can't believe you got through that entire batch of beans before I got back."

Marjorie pointed at Lansing. "Couldn't have done it without Miss Lansing's help."

"I was happy to lend a hand or two. Besides, Marjorie let me revisit a childhood memory."

"Well, thank you for your help," Carmen said. "Especially on my behalf—I was not looking forward to tackling that mound after having to deal with rude people at the grocery store and post office. I swear there must've been a full moon last night, or something," she chuckled. The bell attached to the front door rang out. "Excuse me, that must be our newest guest."

A few moments later, Lansing headed towards her room with the promise of a pot of tea and plate of scones to be delivered shortly. As she approached the front of the house, she heard Carmen speaking to someone. A man in a suit was signing his registration. He was tall, with dark hair, and a scruffy beard. Well, scruffy wasn't truly the correct word—it was as if he spent a great deal of time trimming the beard to make it look neat and unkempt at the same time. Lansing usually didn't give men with facial hair a second glance, but this guy...he made pseudo shabby enticing and erotic.

With the only other guests being well into their seventies, Lansing was happy there was someone who appeared to be closer to her own age. And it didn't hurt that he was nice to look at, as well.

"Are you any relation to Thurman Kingsley?" Carmen asked him.

Lansing stopped mid-stride and froze. From her research into the area, and Silent Cove, she knew Thurman Kingsley had married one of Delilah's daughters.

Mr. Tall, Dark, and Devastatingly Handsome just got more interesting.

4

The Silent Cove Bed and Breakfast was much nicer than the rundown motel Tucker had passed entering Chistine. After the long drive from Boston, and the meeting with the attorney, he was ready to kick back and relax the rest of the evening.

The discussion with Duncan Shakely had been illuminating, to say the least. There was so much about his family history on his father's side Tucker didn't know. Up until then, with virtually no contact outside the occasional Christmas card from his uncle, Tucker rarely even thought about them. He was much closer to his mother's family than the Kingsley side.

A squat man, Shakely had white hair like earmuffs that wrapped around his balding, pink head. He had watery blue eyes and Tucker wondered if that man shouldn't have retired about fifteen years earlier. His office was nice, and he had excellent coffee, which was about the only way Tucker had managed to stay awake during their meeting.

Shakely had gone through some of the legalities associated with the estate. "Walter left nearly everything to your father, Robert, and their sister, Cora. It appears Walter didn't update his will after Cora's death, and since she pre-deceased him, the estate falls to your father. There were a couple of bequeaths to other members of the family—your great uncle Charles, and second cousin, Oliver—but those may also be folded into Robert's portion if both men have already passed, as well." Shakely pulled his glasses down the bridge of his nose and peered at Tucker over the top. "Do you know the whereabouts of Charles or Oliver?"

Tucker stared at the man for a moment. He'd heard of Charles, but couldn't recall if he'd ever met the man. "As far as I know, no one has spoken to Charles for many years."

"And Oliver?"

Oliver was not a name Tucker recalled hearing his father talk about. "I don't know who that is."

"He was your great aunt Agatha's son—although, he left town while very young. It's possible your father never met him—or even knew about him. Oliver was born out of wedlock, and at that time, and in this town, that was quite scandalous. There was lots of rampant speculation about where he had gone, and what happened to him. All I know is that no one has heard from him in a very long time." Shakely sighed and closed the file on his desk. "Well, no matter, I'll see if I can locate him."

Tucker nodded. *Wow, a long lost cousin.* He'd have to email his father and ask if he knew about Oliver.

"These will get you into the house." Shakely slid a set of keys across the desk. "Have you made funeral arrangements yet?"

"No, that's my next stop. I'm not even sure which funeral home he's at."

Shakely chuckled. "You're in Chistine, there's only one funeral home in town. Continue down Main and take a left at Barclay Avenue. You'll see the sign. Godfrey will help you with whatever you need."

An odd, anxious feeling coursed through his body as he left the attorney's office, causing Tucker's chest to rise and fall more heavily than necessary. Was he more upset about his uncle's death than he anticipated? He barely knew the man.

But ever since leaving Duncan Shakely's office, Tucker's mood had taken a turn to a darker place for no apparent reason. By the time he reached Silent Cove Bed and Breakfast, he wanted to get into his room and block out the day. Rushing to rearrange his life, pack a few items, and drive from Boston up to Chistine must have taken a toll on him he hadn't realized.

At least the front desk lady, Carmen, was sweet—and easy on the eyes. "Are you related to Thurman Kingsley?" She handed him the registration to sign.

Scribbling his signature across the line, he muttered, "Yeah, he was my grandfather. Did you know him?"

"Oh, no," Carmen answered with a chuckle. "We just bought this place about a year ago. But your grandmother, Beaulah Kingsley, has ties to this property. Her father, Maurice Cambridge, had the house built."

Out of the corner of Tucker's eye, he caught sight of a woman standing in the hallway, eavesdropping on the conversation. *Small towns...*his father had warned him about how everyone knows everyone else's business.

Most likely due to eavesdropping on conversations.

If Tucker's mood had been better, he might've taken more of an interest in what Carmen was saying. As it was, too much family history had been dumped on him in a short amount of time and he was in no condition to have a discussion about his great grandfather.

"Will you be dining with us tonight?" Carmen asked, and handed him his room key.

The thought of having to potentially socialize with the other guests made Tucker's head pound. "I don't suppose there's any way I could eat in my room…I've had a long day, and could really use some down time to fight this migraine." He rubbed roughly at his temples in the hopes it would relieve some of the pressure.

"Of course," Carmen said. "Just ring me when you get settled and I'll send my husband, Angelo, up with a tray." She placed her hand on the side of her mouth and leaned a little closer to him. "I'll add an after dinner drink, as well. A little scotch should help you get a good night's sleep."

Tucker was impressed. The woman was perceptive and provided that little something extra that made all the difference. He smiled at her, nodded, and headed toward the stairs. When he reached the hallway, he glanced at where the eavesdropper had been standing, but she was gone.

THE MEAL HAD BEEN AMAZING, even in its simplicity. Beef stew and hot homemade rolls slathered in butter. And the promised after dinner aperitif had hit the spot, and made every muscle in Tucker's body relax as the warm spirit washed through him. Crawling into bed had been pure bliss, and he may have been asleep before his head actually hit the plumped pillows.

He wafted in and out of dreams all night. Most featured people he knew—his parents, his co-workers, his crazy ex-girlfriend, even a grade school classmate he hadn't seen in years.

In one, he sat at the kitchen table in his childhood home talking to his father about buying the moon, the room seemed to darken. Day turned instantly to night, but neither man seemed to take much notice of it. It all seemed perfectly normal.

Bright streaming through the window broke up the darkness and caught Tucker's attention. He peered outside while his father counted the many ways purchasing lunar real estate was a bad investment. Tracing the light into the back yard, Tucker noticed it ensconced a little boy with dark hair and hollow eyes.

"Who is that?" Tucker asked, interrupting his father.

Robert Kingsely glanced up at his son. "Who do you mean?"

"The little boy in the back yard." Tucker pointed out the window.

Shaking his head, Robert said, "There's no one out there. You must be mistaken."

"I'm looking *right* at him." Tucker's tone raised an octave or two, irritation spiking through his veins.

"Don't be silly. Come and sit down. Your Uncle Walter will be here in a moment with cookies and beer."

Tucker strutted to the back door. "I'm going out there."

Robert sighed and raised his hands in defeat. "Okay, but don't blame me if all the cookies are gone by the time you get back."

Darting across the grass toward the light, the cool night air nipped at his exposed skin. The darkness closed in on him. He was gaining on the boy, but had absolutely no idea what he would do once he reached the child.

The boy pointed at something over Tucker's shoulder. Slowing, he looked behind him, and caught sight of a dark figure moving closer to them. Tucker peered at the boy. His mouth was moving, but no sound came out. But Tucker knew what the boy was screaming.

Run!

There was no reason for Tucker to fear anything. There was no indication that the figure was going to harm either him or the boy. But he ran, anyway. He ran as if his life depended on it, not completely sure it wasn't.

Adrenaline spiked through his system. His heart pounded in his chest, and his lungs burned with the exertion. Keeping the boy in his sights, he weaved through tall trees. *When had he entered a forest?*

He didn't need to verify that the menacing figure was still behind him. He could feel the entity breathing. Not his actual breath, but as if the inhales and exhales were a beating drum that pulsed through the ground and rattled Tucker's bones.

Breaking into a clearing, Tucker kept his pace, the boy still ahead of him. He couldn't make out anything in front of them. It was a black void—an undefined space. Hands grasped Tucker's arm. He swung his eyes to the side, and gazed at a tall, gangly boy with a nondescript face. Not blank, really. Fuzzy was a better description.

Tucker sprawled onto the ground and lifted his head. The young boy had shoved him to the ground. The lanky figure barreled towards the smaller boy. He grasped the child's arm, and dragged him away.

Tucker strained to see where they had gone.

A cliff. They were too close to the edge. Tucker tried to scramble to his feet. Something unseen held him down. He struggled against the invisible trap, but it was no use. The lanky boy stepped off the edge, his hand still tight around the boy's arm. Both disappeared.

"No!"

Tucker bolted straight up. Confusion coursed through his mind. Where was he? *Still in the forest?* He glanced around. Moonlight streamed through the window, illuminating the room. *Bed.* Not his bed. *Where?* Inn. He had come to the inn.

Leaning against the headboard, he let his head drop back, and he closed his eyes. His heart still pounded in his chest. He took several slow, deep breaths to calm his nerves. What the hell kind of dream was that?

Note to self...don't drink the scotch in this place again. It triggers hallucinations masked as dreams.

Sliding out of bed, he rummaged through his shaving kit until he found the bottle of pain killers. Popping the top, he tossed back two tablets, chasing them with half a bottle of water.

All he had wanted was to have a nice, peaceful sleep that would leave him relaxed and rejuvenated for the next day. Now, he wondered if he dared to risk closing his eyes again. Watching the boys go over the edge of the cliff, and helpless to stop them, had left a cold emptiness in the pit of Tucker's gut.

"It wasn't real," he murmured, and slid back under the covers. "It was just a very bad dream."

He laid in the bed for what seemed like hours, unable to get the visions out of his head. Eventually, he drifted back to sleep until the morning sun woke him.

At least there was nothing *that* scary in the light of day.

5

The dining room was full when Tucker finally made it down for breakfast. A few people sat at the various four top tables, and Tucker considered which elderly couple was closest to being done with their meal. Then he saw her, the eavesdropper from the previous evening, alone at one of the tables. He weaved through the room, pulled out the chair across from her, and sat down.

"Mind if I join you?" He asked, pulling the napkin from his plate and setting it in his lap before she had an opportunity to object.

With a crinkled brow, she peered over the top of her newspaper, and stared at him.

Tucker smiled. "No other tables available."

"Then please have a seat." She smirked and took a sip of her coffee.

A young woman approached the table and poured Tucker a cup of coffee and walked away.

"I saw you," he said, and took a swallow of coffee. *Damn, this town has great coffee.* He peered at his table mate. She narrowed her eyes just slightly. "You were in the hallway when I checked in."

A slight blush flushed her cheeks. "Oh." A smile slid across her face. "Sorry about that. The name Kingsley caught my attention. I'm researching the history of the town and this Inn." She stuck her hand across the table. "Lansing Abbott."

"Tucker Kingsley, but you already knew that," Tucker said with a wink. "So, you're not from here?"

"No, I teach at a small university just south of Boston—Plymouth University. Have you heard of it?" Lansing asked.

He shook his head. "No."

"Not surprising. Not many people outside of Rhode Island have. Come to think of it, I'm not sure many that live in Rhode Island have heard of it." She chuckled, a beautiful grin slid across her face, her eyes dancing with laughter.

"What do you teach?"

"Early American history."

Tucker nodded. He was becoming one of those bobble heads with a spring for a neck, and a stupid smile across his face. Lansing Abbott was captivating. Her long, brown hair fell in soft waves around the tanned, smooth skin across her shoulders and chest. Tucker's eyes dropped to her v-neck t-shirt providing a hint of cleavage.

"I gather you're not from here, either?" She asked.

Tucker tore his eyes from her chest and cleared his throat. "Boston." He was usually a lot better at small talk than this. And definitely more skilled at not getting caught checking out a woman's...assets. But this woman was simply stunning, and intrigued Tucker in a way not many woman had in the past. She didn't come off as embarrassed or offended by him, or his lack of manners. She oozed confidence, grace, and intellect. She seemed to be flipping the tables on Tucker, who was a master of intimidating people with charm and determination. "My father's family is from here, though. In fact, that's why I'm in town. My uncle passed away, and my parents are out of the country. I drew the short straw and have to take care of everything."

Lansing stared at him as if he had the compassion of a medieval executioner. The declaration probably came off a little cold and insensitive in light of a family member passing.

"I wasn't close to this side of the family. In fact, I was pretty young when we stopped visiting here, so I don't have a lot of memories of my uncle. He never came to Boston to see us, and only kept in contact with my father. There was barely any mention of him over the years, and—sad to say—I sort of forgot about him."

Lansing propped her elbows on the table, laced her fingers together, and cradled her chin across them. "There are no other family members that could've taken care of this?"

"Apparently not." Tucker shrugged. "My father is the only surviving sibling. Uncle Walter never married or had children. So, that leaves me."

She gazed at him for a moment, and Tucker wondered if she was trying to think of another question, or judging his flippant attitude toward his uncle.

"Are you having a service for him?" she asked.

"Not sure yet. That's one of the things I have to decide. My uncle requested he be cremated so it's not essential that I make any decisions right now. I'm trying to ascertain if he had friends, or was as aloof to the people in town as he was with the rest of his family.

Although—" Tucker paused, tapped his finger against his chin, and considered his statement, "—I don't know how fair that actually is...I'm pretty sure my father is the one who pulled away from this side of the family."

Why am I telling her my family history? He barely knew this woman and he was spilling his guts to her. God forbid she ask him about his love life—or sex life—he'd probably spill the beans on his decision to remain a bachelor forever. Or how he had sent more than one woman packing with tears streaming down her face after she had demanded some sort of commitment from him.

Marriage was not what Tucker was looking for. He was happy with his single life and prosperous career. His fifth floor condo on Rowe's Wharf with views of Boston Harbor had only one bedroom, and a very small bathroom. Not enough room for a woman—and he had no desire to upgrade. He appreciated being able to come and go as he pleased, go to bars when he wanted, and hang with the boys without being hassled. The thought of having to check in with someone sent a shiver up and down Tucker's spine.

"Seems like you'd want to have some sort of memorial for him. Once you get that out of the way, you can leave town."

Lansing's voice pulled him from his thoughts. *Snap out of it, man! Beautiful woman across from you...pay attention to her.*

She had a nice voice. Not high pitched, or girlie. In fact, it was a little deep for a woman. But not too deep that she could be mistaken for a man. Sensuous and engaging, and it sent a bolt of hot heat through Tucker, straight to his groin.

What the hell?

He cleared his throat and took a swig of coffee. "I

doubt that will happen anytime soon. I'm planning on being here at least a week to clean out my uncle's house and put it on the market to sell."

"Sounds daunting."

He snorted. "I'm not really looking forward to it."

"Would you like some help?" Lansing asked.

Tucker stalled mid swallow, his mouth filled with coffee. Why on earth would this woman he had just met ten minutes earlier want to give up her vacation—sabbatical—to help a man she doesn't know clean the house of a dead man she had never met before?

A smile slid across Lansing's face. "Judging by the look on your face, you're skeptical of my intentions. Let me put you at ease—I'm not some lunatic trying to gain entry into your family home to pilfer it. I only thought since you need help, and I'm doing research on the history of this town, we could both benefit from this alliance. If I understood you correctly, your uncle's family has a long history in Chistine. Who knows what information might be inside the walls of his home."

"Okay, that makes sense. But what makes you think my uncle will have anything of interest to you?"

She chuckled, and the sound was delicious, warming Tucker's belly, and stirring his libido to life. "You'd be amazed at what I find interesting."

Tucker had no doubt, and somewhere in the back of his mind—or perhaps a little more south of his waistband—he hoped they had some similar interests that only involved the two of them.

"Well, Professor Abbott—"

"Dr. Abbott," she corrected him, but then immediately flushed.

Shit, that was fun…she's sexy as hell when she's embarrassed.

"My apologies, *Dr.* Abbott. I'd be happy to have

your assistance. I only ask that anything you find, and decide to use in any publication with respect to my family, be run by me first."

"Deal." She reached her hand across the table, and Tucker shook it, giving it a slight squeeze this time around. *Wonder what she would do if I don't let go?*

"And just for the record," Tucker said. "It wasn't your pilfering that had me worried."

"Do tell."

"I was worried about my virtue, and you robbing me of it."

Her eyes sparkled, and became a deeper shade of green. "I never promised I wouldn't corrupt you."

Tucker laughed. "No," he shook his head, his face nearly in pain from his wide grin. "You certainly did not."

Wow...Dr. Lansing Abbott had done what many women had tried and failed to do—she piqued Tucker's interest. What was it about her that had him suddenly feeling like a goofy teenager with an absurd crush?

The beating of his chest and sweaty palms made his head swim. *This is ridiculous. Women don't unhinge me. I'm the one who agitates women to the point of distraction.*

But Tucker knew one thing...he was excited and wanted to learn more about this woman. Even if it meant having to stay in this one-horse town for longer than he had anticipated.

6

Tucker pulled alongside the curb in front of a quaint white cottage. Lansing figured it had to have been built roughly in the early 1920's.

"Is this it?" She asked.

"Yep." Tucker turned the engine off, released his seatbelt, and opened his door.

"Doesn't look too bad."

Empty cement flower urns sat atop two short stone pillars that flanked the front walk. A bluish-green porch stretched the full length of the house. Lansing wondered if the porch was original to the house. More importantly, she hoped to hell it would hold their weight. Cautiously stepping onto it, she was pleasantly surprised that it seemed quite sturdy with only slight give from the years of salt air and usual wear. In fact, the exterior of the house seemed to be in good repair.

Tucker unlocked the front door and pushed it open. A gush of stall air hit her as she stepped inside. According to the family attorney, no one had been in the house since Tucker's uncle had been removed. Dust tickled her nose and she stifled a sneeze. She had thought it might smell of death, but Uncle Walter must not have been dead for long before he was discovered. *One positive aspect of small towns and nosy neighbors, I guess...*

A red brick fireplace with a wood mantel filled one wall in the small living room. A single chair, a couch, and two tables were the only furniture, and they looked to be about as old as the house. It looked as it probably had for decades and Lansing doubted the room had been used in quite some time. The days of greeting guests and entertaining them in the formal parlor were past. Most people were content to keep social gatherings casual.

A staircase leading to the second floor had a worn banister. Beautiful, and likely original, hardwood floors flowed through the downstairs, as far as she could see.

A doorway to the right opened into a kitchen. Lansing was a little anxious to go in there if food had been left out and was rotting. She could handle a lot of things but maggot-infested food remnants were not among them.

She followed Tucker through a doorway on the left of the stairs. A worn recliner, stacks of paper, and a TV. She'd wager this was where Walter spent most of the time. But it was a bookcase along one wall in the shape of a ship's helm that drew Lansing's interest. It was unlike anything she had ever seen before. The wood trim had been chiseled to look like waves, and the rosettes at the corners carved in the shape of boats. No doubt whittled by hand, the intricate craftsmanship was unrivaled by today's mass production by machines. It was breathtaking, but few people would appreciate the treasure from the past. It was possible new owners would remodel the home and the bookcase would be taken out. Lansing's heart ached a bit, envisioning the unique piece of history splintered and broken, dumped in some landfill instead of being preserved for future generations to enjoy.

She wondered if there was a way to remove the bookcase and maintain the integrity of the piece. Could she convince Tucker to let her try before he put the house on the market? She snorted...*and put it where, Lansing? Your tiny home that's the size of a closet?*

A deep heavy sigh pulled her from her musings. Tucker stood next to a small desk, stack of mail in hand, and sifted through the envelopes. From all appearances, Walter Kingsley did not throw anything away.

"Should we check out the rest of the house?" Lansing asked.

"Yeah, probably," he muttered and dropped the mail back on the desktop.

They passed by two closed doors as they made their way down the hallway beside the staircase. The kitchen looked as if it'd received a facelift in the last ten to fifteen years. The bead board cabinets were all painted white, the walls were yellow, and the backsplash behind the stove had yellow tile interspersed with a few bright red ones, all laid out in a diamond pattern.

A few dirty dishes sat in the sink, but had at least been rinsed off. To Lansing's great relief, there was no rotting food or offensive odors.

So, Walter wasn't a slob, just a hoarder.

Tucker stepped back into the hallway, and opened one of the closed doors into a bedroom. The sheets were ruffled and a blanket was in a heap at the foot of the bed. A few things were strewn across the floor, apparently knocked off the dresser and side table. Lansing knew a neighbor had discovered Walter and called 911. Was this where he had died? The small size of the room would've made it difficult to maneuver a stretcher. Maybe that accounted for things strewn about the room.

Next to the bedroom was a bathroom. The upstairs had three small bedrooms, an even smaller bathroom, and a living area. Boats dotted the harbor, and Lansing decided the deck was the perfect place to take a break.

"This view alone should get you a good price on the house," Lansing said to Tucker.

"It is pretty nice. And quiet. I never realized the value of being in a serene environment until now. It's like taking a deep breath, holding it for a few seconds, and then exhaling every bit of air."

Lansing nodded. That was exactly how she felt. "This spot, with this view—that's the exhale."

"I agree."

They stood for another moment, both silent. Lansing watched the water as it lapped against the sides of the docked boats, mesmerized by their gentle sway.

"Doesn't take much to get lost in the nothingness," Tucker whispered.

Inhaling through her nose, she turned, rejuvenated to commence the task at hand. "Does make facing the daunting family room easier."

Tucker nodded, but his gaze remained on the water. "The sooner we get to it, the sooner we can grab some lunch and sit out on this porch again."

They took opposite sides of the room, Tucker heading back to the desk to sort the mail and look through documents and important papers that might be in the drawers or files. Lansing started with the personal effects on the bookcase. They had decided to divide things into simple piles to begin with—photos and knick-knacks, personal papers, and business-type documents. After the initial sorting, they could get more specific, but this was a good place to start.

A couple of hours into the undertaking, Tucker ran to the cafe and grabbed some sandwiches. While he was gone, Lansing went into the kitchen, and washed the few dishes in the sink. Rinsing the last glass, she set it in the drain rack, and stared mindlessly into the backyard. Walter had done a nice job back there. A stone path meandered toward the rear of the property with beds of wildflowers nestled in each curve. Off to the left was a sitting area with three Adirondack chairs around a fire pit that took full advantage of the spectacular water view.

A shadow in the yard caught Lansing's attention. Standing at the edge where the grass ended and the trees began stood a young boy. Why was he wearing long black shorts, a white button up short-sleeved shirt? The sun was out, but it was still a brisk spring day. Not nearly warm enough out for summer attire. And what boy wore black patent leather shoes to play outside?

She watched him, spellbound by his pale face, deep-set, hollow eyes. The kid had an eery look about him. The shadows from the trees didn't help the haunting allusion, either. There was something about the way he stood stock-still staring at her. He looked...

Lost.

She turned the water off, dried her hands on a dishtowel, and went to see if he needed anything. She opened the side door, stepped out onto the porch, and rounded the corner.

"Hi there." She waved as she proceeded across the grass toward him. There was no reaction from the boy. His eyes never left hers. And she hadn't seen him blink once.

Halfway across the yard, the boy turned and disappeared into the trees.

"Hey," Lansing called to him, but the boy didn't stop. Jogging toward the treeline, she tripped over a broken branch coming up through the grass.

Searching the area, she was sure she would catch a glimpse of him walking through the foliage.

Nothing. *As if he had vanished into thin air*.

"Lansing?"

She yelped. Tucker stood at the corner of the house, his eyebrows drawn together. Waving to him, she took one last glance into the forest, and headed back to the house.

"Why were you on the ground?" Tucker asked.

"I tripped over a branch." She brushed dirt from her knees, thankful she didn't have any discernible grass stains on her pants.

"What were you doing out here in the first place?"

"It was the weirdest thing," she said. "I was washing the dishes and I saw a boy in the yard. I thought maybe he was lost, because he was just staring at me, but by the time I got out here, he was gone."

"Huh…" Tucker looked past her to the trees and shrugged. He held up the brown paper bags. "Lunch is served, if you're still hungry."

Her stomach grumbled as if on cue, and she rubbed her hand over it. "No creepy little kid is going to curb my appetite." She followed Tucker through the house and up the stairs to the upper deck. Comfortably settled into her chair, she took a bite of her lobster roll and groaned in satisfaction. Tucker chuckled, inhaling half of his sandwich. But Lansing couldn't seem to get the backyard visitor out of her mind.

"I wonder who that little boy was?"

He shrugged and shoved a handful of potato chips

in his mouth, chewed, and swallowed. "Probably some neighbor kid wondering who you are."

She hadn't thought of that. From what Lansing could tell, Walter had lived in the house for a very long time. Maybe most of his life. No doubt the neighbors were curious about who she and Tucker were. "Maybe he used to visit Walter, and didn't realize he had died."

"Or doesn't understand what that means." Tucker glanced into the yard. "It can be a difficult concept to understand when you're young."

Lansing agreed. She remembered being told her grandfather had passed away—that he was with the angels—and seven-year-old Lansing had asked when they were going to visit him "in his new home".

"You may be right." She just couldn't place the odd feeling that there was more to the little boy than met the eye. His appearance disturbed her. Not simply that he didn't belong in the yard, but that he didn't belong —*at all*. There was a sense that he was out of place, or time, which made no sense at all.

Tucker crumpled the paper wrapping from his sandwich, and sucked down the remainder of his drink. "I'm going back downstairs, you take your time and relax."

She nodded, and watched the screen door close behind him and latch. She exhaled and rolled her shoulders. The hairs on the back of her neck stood on end.

Someone's watching me.

Peering into the trees, she searched for the little boy. Had he returned? Was he watching her?

Didn't matter. Whoever—or *whatever*—was out there made the blood in her veins turn to ice. Grabbing her trash, she took one last glance into the forest before closing and locking the door behind her.

7

Food was just the jumpstart Tucker needed to tackle the piles of papers that lined the walls of the family room. Lansing had come downstairs not long after he had left her on the upper deck. Her face was pale, and she looked a little queasy. When Tucker asked if she was okay, she simply smiled, and set about sorting the rest of the bookcase items.

After another couple of hours, where the only noise was the shuffling of papers, Lansing pulled out a shoebox from a cabinet that sat along the wall.

"Score!" In her hand she grasped a small black leather-bound book. Her eyes gleamed. "Journal." She placed the book back into the box and set the shoebox aside.

Tucker smiled, not sure how he had managed to be so lucky as to find the one person in town that wanted to dig through someone else's mess. A higher power had definitely been looking out for him when Lansing Abbott was put in his path. Aside from being great company, he was enjoying just *being* with her. She didn't seem to be the type of woman who needed to fill empty space with meaningless chatter. So much of the afternoon had been spent in silence, but it was a comfortable silence, and Tucker felt at ease with this woman he barely knew. That was a brand new experience. He'd had girlfriends he'd been with for months and never felt relaxed around. Lansing was the exception.

At the bottom of a pile of papers he found a large manila envelope. Unclasping it, he peered inside, finding a treasure of his own. He dropped onto the couch, pulled out a few of the photographs, and sifted through them. Lansing plopped down beside him and looked over his shoulder as he went through the stack.

He stared at a black and white photo of two girls and two boys. Turning the photo over, he peered at the date. *1931*. The writing was faded, but he was still able to make out the names. "Beaulah, Agatha, Charles, Calvin."

"Who are they?" Lansing asked.

"Well, Charles is my great uncle, Agatha my great aunt, and Beaulah was my grandmother."

Lansing leaned closer, and Tucker caught a whiff of her unique scent. It was sweet—not flowery, more like vanilla. Whatever it was, it made Tucker want to bury his nose in her hair and breathe her in. *Probably a little too soon for that*.

"Wonder how old they were in this picture?" she asked.

Tucker tried to recall what year his grandmother had been born. "My grandmother would've been about ten years old, which would make Agatha around twelve or thirteen, and Charles—eight?"

"Who is the other boy?" She sat back and Tucker looked more closely at the photo.

"I'm not sure. The name on the back says Calvin, but I don't know any relations with that name."

"Maybe Marjorie will know," Lansing said, covering her mouth as she yawned. "She grew up in the house—the Inn. You could show it to her and see what she says." Scooting to the edge of the couch, she stood. "Maybe it's a long lost relative."

"Just what I need—another wayward family member to track down." Tucker snorted and returned the photos to the envelope. He made sure the picture with the mystery child was on top. "I think we've done enough for one day. Let's get out of here."

"Sounds good. Do you mind if I take this with me," she asked, holding up the journal. "It will give me something to read tonight."

Tucker couldn't imagine anything more boring than reading the diary of someone he'd never met, but who was he to judge? Personally, he could think of about a hundred other things he'd rather do in bed other than read. He stifled a laugh imagining the professor, naked, with her nose in the journal while Tucker thrust into her. "Knock yourself out."

A smile brightened her face, and it was as if the sun kissed her cheeks, emitting rays that bathed Tucker in heat. *Jesus, what is wrong with me? I'm never affected by all this warm, fuzzy shit.*

When they returned to Silent Cove, Lansing grabbed his hand and led him down the hallway. Inside the kitchen, a small elderly woman stood at the sink with her back to them.

"Hi, Marjorie," Lansing said, announcing their presence. "This is Tucker—he's a guest--from Boston."

Marjorie nodded toward them. "How do you do?"

"Fine, thank you." Tucker had no idea how to ask

this woman about the photo. He glanced at Lansing hoping for a little assistance.

Lansing's mouth quirked up on one side. "Tucker's uncle was Walter Kingsley. Did you know him?" she asked.

Thank God she understood that pathetic optic plea for help.

Marjorie's face lit up. "Oh, yes, I was very familiar with the Kingsley family. The older Kingsley's would often come to the house when I was growing up."

Tucker pulled the photo from the envelope. "I found a picture of my grandmother, and her brother and sister. There's another boy in with them—do you know who he is?"

Marjorie stared at the photo, her eyes narrowing in concentration. "Oh, yes…I remember him. Quiet boy, was about the same age as Charles, I believe. Maybe a year or two younger."

"Is his name Calvin?" Tucker said. "It's written on the back."

"Yes," Marjorie said, nodding. "I remember now. I didn't know him, but he must've been very good friends with Charles because he always accompanied the Kingsley children when they came to visit."

"Didn't you talk to him—or play with them when they were here?" Lansing asked.

Marjorie shook her head. "Not really. Mother would only let me play with Agatha and Beaulah—and only inside the house. She said it wasn't proper for a young lady to play with boys. She was very strict about my outside play, as well, restricting me to the gardens. I was never allowed to venture back into the trees. Of course, Agatha and Beaulah didn't want to stay inside with a girl half their age, so they would usually follow the boys back outside after they had a snack."

"But you don't know who this boy is?" Tucker asked, pointing to Calvin. "His last name, maybe?"

"No, I'm terribly sorry. Mother never mentioned his family. After a time, the Kingsley children stopped coming here. My mother had a falling out with William's widow, Zora Sue, and the kids never returned. I don't recall ever seeing Calvin after that, not even when we went to town."

"That's odd," Lansing said.

Marjorie shrugged. "Mother kept me pretty sheltered out here. After all that took place, with the murders of Eliza and Maurice, and Delilah and William dying, people in town thought the place was cursed. I guess they figured since we remained on the property, we were cursed, too."

Marjorie handed the photo back to Tucker. "I'm sorry I couldn't be more help."

"You were a great help," Lansing corrected the woman.

"Yes, thank you," Tucker said. "I know so little about this side of my family, any information I can get is appreciated."

Marjorie smiled at him, her eyes watery. "You are as handsome as your father, Robert. I was sad when he left town…such a nice young man. Always so polite."

Tucker wasn't sure what to say. "Thank you," he mumbled.

Lansing grabbed his hand. "We'll let you get back to what you were doing. Thank you so much, Marjorie." Tucker liked her hand in his, which was odd. He was never much for public displays of affection, but holding hands with Lansing Abbott sent a thrilling jolt through him.

What is it about this woman?

Once they had reached the foyer, Tucker tugged on

her hand. "So, do you want to tell me about what she meant by deaths and murders?"

"Yes, but right now, I need a shower and clean clothes. Do you want to eat dinner together? I can fill you in on what I know."

Tucker suddenly felt every bit of dust and dirt on his skin, and he itched to get out of his clothes and under the hot water spray. "Sounds like a date." They walked up the stairs together, and Tucker watched Lansing peel away toward her room at the end of the hall.

He rubbed the growth along his cheek as she disappeared into her room. Too bad they couldn't conserve water and take a shower together. Sudsy, soapy, naked Lansing under his hands—what would that be like? He nearly groaned at the thought.

Damn intriguing woman.

8

"I was thinking about what you told me last night—" Tucker said, placing his napkin in his lap as his breakfast plate was laid before him. He thanked the waitress, and then leaned over the table closer to Lansing—"about all the g-h-o-s-t's around here." His voice lowered to just above a whisper.

Lansing smiled, but forced back the giggle. It wasn't that long ago that she'd had a hard time wrapping her head around the ethereal residents of the Inn. Within a couple of days, though, they seemed a foregone conclusion.

"And what have you decided?" she asked, breaking into her soft-boiled egg nestled in the delicate porcelain cup. She had explained everything she knew about the old inn, the stories she had read on the website, and the information she had gleaned from Carmen and Marjorie. To his credit, Tucker had taken it all in and waited until she was done to snicker at her. She knew it wasn't meant to be derogatory—which was all that saved him from getting a tongue-lashing about being rude—and hoped that a good night's sleep would help him be more open to the prospect.

Tucker inhaled deeply through his nose. "I'm not sure I'm completely convinced they exist, but I'm willing to give the notion the benefit of the doubt. I would, however, like to see the gravestone under the tree. Can you show me?"

"Sure. And for the record, if I hadn't seen Eliza with my own eyes, I might not have believed the stories about this place either."

After breakfast, Lansing and Tucker walked through the gardens and along the trail into the woods. At the bend, she pointed to the base of the big tree. "That's it," she said, and wondered why she was shocked that it was still there. Did she subconsciously believe someone would remove it because she had asked about it?

The weirdness that existed on the property seemed to make any ludicrous outcome a possibility.

A large man was kneeling next to the stone, cleaning away the debris that had fallen from the tree limbs above. He glanced up at the couple as they came to a stop beside him.

"Hi," Lansing said.

"Hello," the man answered, and went back to his work. He must have assumed his cold acknowledgement would encourage them to move on down the path, because he glanced up at them with narrowed eyes and a quizzical brow.

"We're staying here at the inn." She pointed behind her to the large house, as if he might be confused about what inn she meant. "My name's Lansing."

The man nodded. "How do you do, ma'am?"

"Just fine, thank you." She grabbed a hold of her companion's arm. "This is my friend, Tucker."

Then it was Tucker's turn to nod.

Men!

"Tucker Kingsley." Lansing drew out his last name. The man's eyes widened, and his gaze flew to Tucker. "And you're William?"

Not taking his eyes off Tucker, he nodded, and said, "Yes, ma'am." Standing, he wiped his hands on his pants. "Are you Robert's son?" he directed to Tucker.

"Yes, sir." Tucker's face paled as recognition seemed to hit him that this was one of the many otherworldly entities on the estate. And this one—his great, great grandfather—knew his family very well, most likely better than Tucker knew them.

"How is he?" William asked. He glanced down the trail toward the inn. "Is he here?"

"No, I'm afraid he and my mother are on a trip and won't return for several months. I'll be handling Walter's estate."

"Oh," William replied, his voice low and quiet. "Well, it's nice that you were able to take care of things."

"I'm happy to be able to help. I haven't been here since I was young—I mean, to Chistine. This is my first visit to...well, here...the inn." He shifted his weight back and forth on his feet.

"I'm sure that's true," William acknowledged. "But you look just like your father the last time I saw him—and you favor Beaulah very much, as well." William smiled which crinkled the corners of his eyes as they lifted.

"I remember Grandma Beaulah," Tucker said. "She would make maple walnut cookies the size of my hand." Both men chuckled.

"That was my wife's, Zora Sue—your great, great grandmother—recipe. The kids would fight to get one as soon as they came out of the oven."

Lansing's heart warmed. She was privy to an amazing moment to witness. How many people can say they have met their great, great grandfather? And to see the joy this meeting was giving William, whom she would bet didn't smile or find joy in much over the years, brought tears to her eyes. She touched her finger to the corner of each eye to stop any from spilling over and running down her cheeks.

Tucker glanced at Lansing, and for a moment it looked as if he just remembered she was present. The three stood in silence for a moment.

William twisted his cap in his hand. "Well, suppose I ought to get back to work."

"Before you go," Lansing asked, reaching out for him, but stopping before making contact with his arm. She remembered from reading the information on the website that he was unable to have contact with the living. "Can you tell us whose grave this is?"

He shook his head, and a frown darkened his face. "Not a grave," he said a little too forcefully. "Just a rock."

"But there's a date—" Lansing pointed at the rock.

"No, not a grave." He was almost angry at the implication. "Not a date."

What the hell?

"Okay," Lansing said, and kept her tone calm. Nothing would be served by upsetting William. Her curiosity was piqued, and she wanted answers that she knew she was going to have to needle out of him. "I was here the other day, and I saw Eliza standing here."

William's head jerked in her direction. She'd swear flames burned in his eyes. "Stay away from that woman. Nothing good ever comes from being around her."

"But—"

Without another word, William turned and stalked away.

Lansing pivoted in Tucker's direction. The encounter with William made her head reel. "What the hell was that all about?"

"I don't know," Tucker said, looking down the path in his great, great grandfather's direction. "But he's certainly adamant that this is not a grave."

"A little too adamant."

Tucker nodded. "That's what I was thinking." He grabbed a hold of Lansing's hand and turned them back toward the Inn. "Looks like we have a bit of a mystery on our hands. I don't know about you, but this whole encounter has made me hungry. Let's see if Marjorie has a midmorning snack."

"I need coffee," Lansing added. "With a shot of whiskey."

9

Tucker sat across from Duncan Shakely as the man shuffled through paperwork on his desk. Lansing was waiting for him at the diner in town and Tucker wanted to be with her more than anything. The feeling unsettled him. Tucker usually let women pine for him, and had yet to find one he yearned for...until he met the intriguing Dr. Abbott.

Duncan cleared his throat, and Tucker decided to delve into his craving for Lansing later. He needed to deal with Uncle Walter's estate first. Then he would consider how to get the good doctor into bed.

Sliding a document across the desk, Shakely pointed at the bottom. "Sign here." When Tucker had finished, Duncan said, "The house is all yours. I'll get the new deed recorded this afternoon." He placed the document into the file and set it on the corner of his desk. "Any idea what you'll do with the property?"

"Probably put it on the market," Tucker said. "Although my main focus is getting it cleared out and then seeing where to go from there. I'd like to talk to my dad about it, also, and find out if he wants to keep it."

"That house has been in your family for generations. Your great, great grandfather had it built for his wife, Zora Sue. He was a fisherman and gone most of the time, so he wanted Zora and the kids to have a nice home. From what Walter told me, it was Zora Sue who insisted it have a view of the bay so she could watch for him, and he could see them as he was leaving and returning home." Duncan smiled. "Not sure how true that is, but it's quite romantic, don't you think?"

Tucker nodded. Apparently the older a man gets, the more inclined toward finding things romantic he becomes. Tucker was not really into romance—in fact, he'd been told by more than one woman that he sucked at it—so recognizing it and acknowledging it were somewhat foreign to him.

The best thing to do was to change the subject, or at least the focus of the conversation. Practicality needed to rule the day. He had too much to get through.

And he wanted to get back to Lansing.

Which is somewhat romantic. What the hell is up with me?

He shook his head to rid himself of the awkward pressure growing in his chest. "So, the house has been passed down and no one outside the family ever owned it?"

"After Zora Sue passed away, she left it to Beaulah. Delilah had been dead for many years, so everything passed to her grandchildren. By then Agatha had died—quite tragically—and no one had heard neither hide nor hair of Charles. Beaulah kept the house, and gave it to her three kids. When Walter returned from the Army, he and your aunt Cora moved into it. Your father moved to Boston to go to college, and I don't think he ever lived there."

"Delilah died at Silent Cove, from what I understand."

"Yes," Duncan sighed and shook his head. "Horrible death."

"I heard she swan-dived off the second floor balcony after shooting her husband and his mistress."

Shakely frowned. A creased lined his forehead. "True. She'd lived with Maurice's philandering for years, but I guess she finally had enough. I often wonder—if she had known the outcome—whether or not she would have gone through with it."

"What do you mean?" Tucker asked. He had heard the story of Maurice, Eliza and Delilah's deaths from Lansing, but was curious if Shakely had other information.

"Well, her father tried to prevent Delilah from killing Maurice and Eliza. He was too late, though. By the time he arrived, Delilah had shot her husband and Eliza, and then committed suicide. Poor William had a heart attack when he saw his daughter. Died right next to her in the ballroom."

"Right, William—I met him," Tucker said.

"Excuse me?"

Tucker jerked his head up. Duncan stared at him, one eyebrow cocked. Realizing the mistake he had made, Tucker scrambled to cover his blunder. He knew people in town thought the inn was odd, but wasn't sure they understood the extent of paranormal activity on the property. "I read about him. Walter has about a million newspaper from when they first started printing them, I think." He chuckled and hoped he had adequately covered his fuck up. "What happened to Charles?"

"I'm not sure," Duncan drew out, leaning back in his chair. "He was the youngest of Delilah's kids. I know he went into the Army. When he returned, he married a local girl, Penelope Grayson. They lived here for a while...I heard there were problems with her being able to have kids. They eventually left town, and never returned. No one knows where they are, or if they're still alive."

A shiver ran down Tucker's spine. How was it possible no one knew where Charles and Penelope had gone or if they had died? "Not even Penelope's family?"

"If they know, they have remained very tight-lipped about it. I talked to her sister and niece after Walter passed, but they both deny knowing Penelope's whereabouts."

"Odd," Tucker said.

"That's Chistine, for you," Duncan said, and finished his coffee. "No shortage of strange things happening here."

10

Lansing stepped inside Jazzy's Diner, a small cafe located on the main drag in Chistine, and was immediately swept up in 1950's atmosphere. She wondered if everything was original. If so, the place had been kept in immaculate condition. Bustling with morning breakfast patrons, some looking as if they were original to the place, as well.

Lansing draped the strap of her computer bag over the back of the stool and sat at the counter. She inhaled the scent of bacon. A young woman in a pink and white uniform stopped in front of her, bright smile on her face, and a pot of coffee in her hand. Her nametag read Lindsey. "Coffee?"

"Please." Lansing sighed, flipped her cup over, and inhaled the deep aroma of the brew. "Thank you so much."

"Of course. Would you like to look at the breakfast menu?"

"No." Lansing's gaze flitted along the counter to the cover glass pedestals at the opposite end. "What kind of pies do you have?"

"So far this morning, cherry and apple."

"Slice of cherry, please." Lansing salivated at the thought of one of her favorite desserts as a child. Often Lansing's mother would make one for her birthday in lieu of cake.

"Ice cream or whipped cream?"

"Neither, but could you heat it up for me?"

"Of course." Lindsey bounced away, her long ponytail swaying as she walked.

A couple of seats down from Lansing, an older woman folded up her napkin, and tossed it on top of her plate. She had dark hair streaked with grey, pulled back into a ponytail. The frizzy split ends indicated it should've been hacked off twenty years earlier.

Lindsey slid the pie onto the counter in front of Lansing. She sliced her fork through the end. The burst of tartness as she bit into a cheery mixed with sweet warmth and spread across her tongue.

"You're not from around here," the older woman stated. It wasn't a question, which wasn't all that surprising in a small town like Chistine. Some of these families had been among the first settlers in the area. New people stuck out like a pimple on picture day.

Lansing pulled a few paper napkins from the metal dispenser in front of her. "No, just visiting."

The woman snorted. "No one ever visits Chistine."

Lindsey passed by with a plate of eggs and hash browns. "Don't be silly. Now that the bed and breakfast is open, we have lots of visitors coming to town on vacation. Although, I can't imagine why anyone would pay money to stay there."

The old woman crossed her arms over her chest and harrumphed. "That inn has been opened and closed so many times, it's a wonder someone hasn't installed a revolving door for the owners to come and go."

"I've heard it's had problems over the years," Lansing said. "But I think the current owners have things under control."

The woman scowled. "Until they don't."

Lansing couldn't argue with her. So far, the quaint yet quirky bed and breakfast had been a great place to stay. Of course, Lansing's interest in the place may be slightly different than the usual guests. She had no interest in strolling the grounds, relaxing under a tree in the garden, or taking a tour of a retired fishing boat. The otherworldly aspects of the town were the only reasons she had decided to stay there.

But it might not be the only reason she was staying. A vision of Tucker with a sexy smirk on his face sent her heart galloping. There was something about him that gripped her interest and wouldn't let go. She'd had relationships with men outside of the academic world where she resided. Nothing worked out. Grading papers, coming up with new lesson plans, and trying her damnedest to get the next book published were top priorities. Men with nine-to-five desk jobs demanded she be available nights and weekends. Something she often couldn't do. Or was it that she hadn't met a guy she had wanted to do that for?

No matter, Tucker was part of corporate life.

Of course, just because none of her previous relationships with businessmen worked out didn't necessarily mean this one was doomed to fail. After all, *none* of her relationships so far had worked out, whether the guy was in academia or not.

Wait! Why was she even considering a relationship with Tucker? Aside from a few flirtatious remarks and glances, along with a little innocent handholding, Tucker had made no indications he wanted *any* type of relationship with her.

Way to jump the gun there, Lansing.

"Sylvia Burnham."

Lansing snapped her attention back to the older woman, who had slid onto the seat next to Lansing and quirked up an eyebrow.

Lansing sat there with what had to have been something akin to a deer in headlights look.

"It's nice to meet you. Lansing Abbott." The words rushed out of her mouth as she shook hands with Sylvia. Lansing picked up her fork and sliced off a hunk of pie in an attempt to move past the awkward moment.

"And what brings you to our little corner of paradise?"

"I'm doing research on historical towns in this area. I'm a history professor, but I'm on sabbatical, at the moment." She took a bite of pie and washed it down with coffee.

"Why on earth did you pick this place?" Sylvia asked, and shook her head as a wide grin spread across her face.

"Seemed like a good place to start," she chuckled. "I'm actually helping a friend clear out his uncle's home who recently passed away. Walter Kingsley—did you know him?"

"It's a small town, everybody knows everybody, sometimes too much. I went to school with Robert, Walter's brother."

"My friend, Tucker, is Robert's son."

Sylvia nodded. "At one time, I wouldn't have minded if Walter had been sweet on me. He never was, though, and then I met my Henry." She elbowed Lansing playfully in the ribs and cackled. "Dodged a bullet there, I can tell you."

The statement, and the sharp elbow in her side, took Lansing by surprise. "What do you mean?"

Sylvia stared straight into Lansing's eyes. A grim line replaced her smile. "That family is cursed."

"You don't really believe that, do you?" Lansing chuckled.

Sylvia tapped on the rim of her coffee mug as Lindsey passed by. "How would you explain everything that's happened to them? Delilah kills her husband along with that floozy he was with. Then offs herself. Her poor daddy dies right next to her." She paused as her cup was refilled. "And then there's poor Agatha. Fate worse than death, that one."

Lansing's breath caught. *Someone who knew Agatha.* "Delilah's daughter?"

"Yeah, that's the one…went plum crazy. Wandering around the streets, muttering that a boy was after her, and was going to kill her." Lansing dropped back in her seat before she was hit in the face. Sylvia talked with her hands and was inordinately expressive. "My mother had a women's bible study at our house once a week when I was young. They did a lot more gossiping than praying, I can tell you—"

Lansing tittered quietly to herself. She had known Sylvia all of ten minutes and was getting some very juicy gossip. *Like mother, like daughter.*

"—anyway, on many occasions they would talk about Agatha losing her grip on reality. She was constantly telling Charles and his wife, Penelope, they were cursed. Agatha would tell anyone who would listen that some boy told her that he had killed all the babies in Penelope's womb." Sylvia's tone dropped low and quiet, as if she was providing Lansing with a dark family secret.

Lansing's forkful of pie stalled midway to her mouth. "That's horrible." She couldn't imagine having to go through the pain of a miscarriage and then having to hear that some strange curse was to blame for it. Must have been downright depressing for Penelope, and dammed impossible to spend any amount of time with her sister-in-law. Let alone face people in town that had heard Agatha's strange proclamations.

"Poor Penelope. She was a young wife and tried hard to get along with Agatha. And she was so desperate to have a baby, but time and time again she would be devastated at the loss." Sylvia puffed out her cheeks. "Some of the yahoos in this town actually started taking heed of Agatha's dribble, and would avoid Penelope when they saw her, thinking her bad luck was contagious." Sylvia waved her hand in the air as if shooing away the ridiculous notion. "I guess that's what finally drove Charles and Penelope away. They didn't even come back for poor Agatha's funeral."

"How did Agatha die?" Lansing knew the answer, but wanted to get the full story from Sylvia. No doubt the woman would have some tale Lansing couldn't get from newspaper accountings.

"Depends on who you ask. Most people are content to believe the nutjob jumped off that cliff to get the voices out of her head. A few say she was murdered— rumors still fly around about drag marks where she went over."

Lansing drew in a sharp breath. Murder?

Nothing Lansing had uncovered had hinted at any other cause of death besides suicide. "Did the police investigate it?"

"Not so far as I know. There was talk of a conspiracy —that the family covered it up so as not to have further negative attention on them." Sylvia had both hands wrapped around her mug and was staring intently into the dark liquid.

"But you don't believe either of those theories?"

Sylvia shrugged. "Could be both are true."

A cold wave swept through Lansing. She peered at the woman for a moment before she spoke. "Both? How's that possible?"

Sylvia slid her gaze over to Lansing. "Maybe her ramblings about a little boy trying to kill her came true. Maybe she couldn't take it anymore and went to the bluff, confronted the boy, and he helped her over the edge." Sylvia put her hands in front of her and made a pushing motion.

A shiver ran down Lansing's spine. Could a boy push a grown woman to her death? And, if so, why? She knew it was possible for kids to be evil. Was this mysterious boy an up-and-coming serial killer? That didn't seem plausible. There were no other murders in the area that Lansing had heard of. Unless the boy left town after he killed Agatha, and commenced his killing spree somewhere else.

"Did anyone ever figure out who the boy was?" Lansing asked.

Sylvia slowly wagged her head from side-to-side. "No one ever saw a boy around her."

"So, if it wasn't a boy from town, who do you think he was? Could he have been from somewhere else?"

"Perhaps," Sylvia said. "Maybe it was a boy that lived on the Cambridge property." She paused, as if considering her next words carefully. "Maybe he's still there." Her voice was almost a whisper.

"Do you mean one of the ghosts rumored to be on the estate?"

"Strange things have happened on that property. People talk in a small town and there is no lack of embellishments in most stories. When one person talks, it's easy to dismiss what they say as ridiculous. Two people? Gets a little harder, but could still be a coincidence. But a handful of people that don't know one another…the unbelievable starts looking possible."

Lansing didn't want to tell the woman she'd already come face-to-face with a couple of those unbelievable situations. A week ago she was skeptical of ghosts and hauntings. Now, accepting the impossible as plausible wasn't such an oddity.

Lansing talked with Sylvia for a few minutes longer until the woman hopped off the stool and declared she had things she must get done—number one on her list was an "afternoon siesta". Lansing smiled as she watched the older woman waddle out the door and down the sidewalk.

"Can I get you anything else?" Lindsey asked. Lansing glanced around the nearly empty diner.

When had the placed cleared out?

She must've been more involved in her conversation with Sylvia than she thought.

"More coffee, and another slice of pie."

Lansing didn't need more pie, but thought it was better to order something more than coffee if she was going to be in the diner half the day. "Do you mind if I take up a table?" She pointed to one by the window. "I have some work to do on my laptop and need a little room to spread out."

"No, not at all." Lindsey waved her hand in the air. "I'll bring your coffee and pie right over."

Opening her laptop, Lansing connected to the internet through her cell phone hotspot. Now to find out what happened to the mysterious Charles Cambridge. No one could just disappear off the face of the earth these days. Could they? She typed Charles' name into the Google search bar. Surely, there was some record of his death—an obituary, newspaper article—something that would give Lansing information about his suspicious demise.

The only websites that popped up were public records searches. After going through a couple of pages that showed no real information about the man, Lansing decided to bite the bullet and pay for an online search. While she waited for any information, she looked through the archives of some of the local newspapers in the area. She loved reading small town newspapers. The information contained in them was unlike what she found in the larger publications from Boston, or even Providence. Small towns concerned themselves with bake sales, hospital fundraisers, church schedules, and who had been arrested for tying one on at the local bar. Big city periodicals were filled with murders and rapes and politicians gone bad.

The draw of a simpler life that existed in small towns had its merit. Could Lansing actually live in a place like Chistine?

She checked her email and was delighted to find a response from the search. Opening the documents, she found she had the birth certificate, marriage license, and current address for Charles Cambridge. But no death certificate.

The last known address was in Middleton, about an hour's drive away. Lansing pulled up the Middleton county clerk's website and searched for Charles' death certificate. Nothing. Then she went through the websites for the four funeral homes in the town, and searched for any mention of his name. Nothing again.

A quick search of the local newspaper's archives was the third strike. She was officially out of ideas.

Why would Penelope tell her family that her husband had died when there was no documentation to support the claim? Did she really not want anyone from Chistine trying to find them? It was possible she thought the best way to avoid unexpected guests was to spread a rumor that Charles had died. Seemed a bit morbid but perhaps the couple really didn't want family or friends from Chistine involved in their lives.

Did they actually believe Agatha's ramblings that they were cursed?

What if Charles was dead but still living in the home with his wife? A shiver ran up and down Lansing's spine. While it was upsetting, she wasn't sure what part was more disturbing the thought of a dead body in a home for any length of time, or the real possibility of it being a fact, especially given the history surrounding the Cambridge and Kingsley families.

The bell on the door jingled. Lansing looked up in time to see Tucker walk in and glance around. When his gaze caught hers, a broad smile spread across his face, and something deep in Lansing stirred awake and sent butterflies fluttering in her belly. She couldn't deny that she was getting a charge out of spending time with Tucker. Not only because he was affording her the opportunity to research the town's paranormal history up close and personal, but because she truly enjoyed being around him. He was handsome and funny, smart and successful, but something about him fascinated her like no man had in a very long time.

"Hey," he said as he approached and dropped onto the seat across from her. Lansing knew he had news by the gleam in his eye. She had already come to appreciate the familiarity of him.

"Hey, yourself," she responded, and inhaled the scent of his soap and *him*. It shrouded her like a favorite sweater. "How was your meeting?"

"Interesting. I learned a lot about my family and the history of not only Walter's house, but my great uncle, Charles." He glanced around the diner. "Sorry to have kept you waiting so long, though."

"No, it was actually good that you were gone."

Tucker quirked an eyebrow.

Lansing chuckled. "I met a very chatty woman who knows your family. She told me all about your Aunt Agatha's death."

"How about we order some lunch to go, and head over to Walter's house for the afternoon. We can compare notes while we work."

Lansing closed out of the open screens and logged off the laptop. "Sounds like a great idea."

11

The upper porch at the back of Walter's home had become a favorite place to sit, relax, and eat. And if Tucker was going to be completely honest with himself, he loved the idea of he and Lansing having a special spot all their own. That, in and of itself, was illuminating, warming, and somewhat uncomfortable. He didn't do romance and cutesy couple activities. He liked spending time with women, as long as they enjoyed what he enjoyed. Rarely was it the other way around.

Now—with Lansing—he wanted to know what she liked to do. He wanted to find things they both enjoyed. Discover if they had more common interests than not. In short, he wanted to spend time with Lansing, and didn't much care what the hell they were doing. If the activity meant he could be around her, he was all in.

The most revealing aspect was that they *did* enjoy the same things. After all, she didn't know him before he arrived at Silent Cove. Now, she was completely immersed in his family history. Yeah, she was getting good information for her book research, but she was sort of going above and beyond. She could have gotten the information from him by buying him a nice dinner in town. He would've told her whatever she wanted to know. There wasn't a tight connection with this side of his family, and he felt no loyalty to keep their secrets. But Lansing was at Walter's, giving up her time to go through an old man's home, helping Tucker get the house ready to sell when she could've been sightseeing, or taking day trips on the water. Damn near anything sounded more appealing to Tucker than going through nearly a hundred years of crap his father's family had managed to hoard for no apparent reason.

Tucker wasn't sure he'd have done the same if the tables were turned.

Well—maybe he would for Lansing Abbott. His heart rate kicked up a notch.

What is it about this woman?

WHILE THEY ATE, Tucker explained everything Shakely had told him about the house, and Lansing relayed what Sylvia had said about Agatha.

"Do you think it's possible that Agatha drove them away from Chistine?" Tucker asked.

Lansing had been pondering the same question. "It might've been. According to Sylvia, Penelope was stressed about getting pregnant, which may have caused the miscarriages. Perhaps they felt they needed to escape. But would Charles really want to cut all ties with his family?"

"If Charles was fed up with his family, he could've decided to get Penelope away from everyone, *including* her family. Small town—everyone knows everything about their neighbors secrets."

True. Lansing stared out over the water. She could get used to spending time up here, mesmerized by the gentle sway of the water, immersed in watching the fishermen unload their daily haul of fish and lobsters. "So, is Penelope trying to return the favor for Charles by telling his family he died? It seems odd that I haven't been able to find any information about his death."

"What if they were abroad?" Tucker asked. He shifted in his seat to face her. "If they were vacationing overseas, maybe Penelope decided to leave his body wherever they were instead of bringing it back. Or maybe she had him cremated."

Lansing had to admit that was a possibility. The Cambridges' were not short on funds. From what Tucker had told her, Maurice Cambridge established sizable trust funds for his children. Enough that none of them would've had to work, if they'd chosen not to.

"It's very strange…but, people often do things that don't make any sense."

Tucker faced the water again and sighed. "It's easy to judge other people's decisions when you're on the outside looking in."

THEY SAT, taking in the view of the back yard. Huge maples lined the perimeter of the property, with a few chestnut trees scattered throughout the yard. The beginning sprouts of hydrangea, and the promise of daffodils preparing to bloom dotted the landscape. The scent of the sea wafted in from the bay, and provided a cool breeze not really needed even though the sun was shining directly on them. The early spring sun was not hot enough yet for them to be sweltering and in need of cooling off.

Lansing rested her head along the back of the chair, her eyes closed. She looked peaceful and relaxed, and Tucker couldn't help wondering what it'd be like to spend many days like this with her. He'd never considered a long-term relationship, and this one was doomed before it could even be seriously considered. He lived in Boston. She was a professor at a small private college in Rhode Island. Neither one of them belonged in Chistine.

This was just a brief moment in time. A coincidence. A lucky break.

The thought of their time together coming to an end made Tucker's heart seize painfully in his chest. Nothing felt more right than being there with her.

"Where is that wonderful smell coming from?" she asked, without lifting her head or opening her eyes.

Tucker glanced around the yard. On the right side of the house stood a large magnolia tree with new buds on it. "Maybe the magnolia—although it seems early for that to have smell."

"Could be." Lansing sighed and settled back into her chair. "It smells more like ginger to me."

Tucker inhaled deeply and held the breath in. There was something fresh in the air, but he couldn't place the smell. He dropped his head back and closed his eyes. "Could be," he mimicked.

When was the last time he had just sat around and relaxed? Or enjoyed doing nothing more taxing than breathing in and out at regular intervals? His mind was blank—and he was perfectly okay being in that state. Had he ever found joy in the subtle scents of spring before now?

No, not that he could recall, anyway. His life in Boston was chaotic fun. Never standing still for long, moving from one social event to the next. He woke in the morning eager to get to work. Success in his career was a top priority to him. Was it strange that he hadn't thought much about his job since getting to Chistine?

Being active was not just a part of his life, it *was* his life. But now—here with Lansing—it was different. He saw things in a new light, and appreciated things he previously scoffed at.

The simple life. *Why didn't that scare the crap out of him like it had in the past?*

A large part was due to the beautiful woman next to him.

He reached over, grasped Lansing's hand, and held it. "I don't think I've told you how much I appreciate all your help. I don't know how I would've been able to get through all this without you pitching in."

Silence filled the space between them, and then she returned the squeeze. "You're very welcome, but I should be thanking you. I doubt my trip would've been half as exciting if I hadn't met you. Being able to delve into your family's history in this town has tapped into my geeky history professor brain, and even satisfied some of my little exercised paranormal interests. And you haven't rolled your eyes at me or given me a 'you're weird' look once—at least that I've witnessed."

"I like your geeky, paranormal weirdness," Tucker murmured without thinking. "It's makes you quite appealing."

"Appealing?" she asked.

Oh hell, had he just said that out loud?

He looked into her eyes. *Damn, she's pretty.* Warmth slid through his veins like a hot gush of water. She made him want to snuggle up and cuddle and fuck her senseless, but wasn't exactly sure which urge was stronger. She had done the impossible—she made him feel something deeper than natural male horniness. "It's not every day a guy meets a history professor who doesn't bore him to tears talking about some apparently meaningful moment in history."

"Wow, glowing praise," she snorted, a wide grin across her face. "I'm encouraged that I haven't bored you to death."

"To tears," he corrected. "And so am I." He winked, and stood. He needed some distance from her before he kissed the living daylights out of her. There was still so much work to be done in the house. He knew starting something with Lansing would develop into more. And he planned on exploring more with her someplace other than his uncle's dirty dank house. "I'm heading inside before I fall asleep out here and decide to sell the house as is, clutter and all."

Lansing sighed and stretched her arms over her head. "I'm not sure how I will function in life after spending time on this porch. I actually can't remember ever feeling so…relaxed." She chuckled. Flutters hit Tucker's gut with a vengeance. Jesus, he loved the sound of her laugh.

"I know what you mean. I have a new appreciation for having a place in a secluded area. I've never wanted a vacation home before and would make fun of my married friends who would buy one to escape the city." He pulled open the screen door, but looked back out over the yard to the cove. There was something magical in the way the sunlight hit the water—as if diamonds sat on the surface, enticing fishermen to set out on the ocean. He could definitely see the appeal of living along the coast. "Maybe I should just keep this place. Come down here when I need to get away."

"Maybe you should. It is a great location, and the house isn't so big that you couldn't maintain it from a distance."

"True," he agreed. "Maybe I'll swing by and pick you up so you can get away, also."

"*Maybe* I'd like that. Although, Plymouth U is not exactly on the way to Maine—it's in the opposite direction."

"For you, I'll make the detour."

She smiled and looked down at her feet, and that little bit of encouragement sent a spike of something unfamiliar through him. *What is that?* Contentment laced with excitement? Whatever it was, his mind was flooded with visions of what could be. They were gone in a flash, but the story they portrayed made Tucker's heart race—not with the usual fear of commitment he normally had when faced with this sort of situation, but want and desire to actually have what his mind had conjured.

Happily ever after...with one person.

He shook his head. The salt air must be getting to him. Learning about a family he never knew and facing mortality was making him soft. No doubt when he returned to Boston and his normal routine, along with the plethora of women who wanted to be with him, all of these thoughts would be the punchline to a funny joke.

I remember that one time I actually wanted to settle down...it lasted all of one week, then I pulled my head out of my ass. His buddies would howl and hold their sides at the thought of Tucker Kingsley even considering *'til death do us part*.

Except the thought of not having that very thing wasn't what pulled at Tucker's heart and caused his breath to come in short, quick gasps. The prospect of not having any sort of relationship with Lansing made his stomach twist in a knot.

Lansing Abbott had Tucker's insides doing flips.

How the hell did he make it stop?

The bigger question...did he want it to stop?

TUCKER CLOSED the drawer of the desk and sighed. One more drawer cleared out of the mammoth desk. He hadn't found anything really interesting, and tossed most of the papers into the recycle bin. He'd have to see if there was someplace in town that had a shredder. He briefly considered buying one, but after seeing the mounds of papers to shred, figured his time was better spent doing something else. *Anything else.*

Taking a deep breath, he pulled the drawer open, expecting it to be packed with hanging files. To his surprise—and elation—there were only a few folders lying in the bottom. He lifted them out, and dropped them on top of the desk. A large photo album sat in the bottom of the drawer. He balanced the album on his lap and flipped open the cover. Inside newspaper articles had been cut out and placed under the cellophane.

The first page had a picture of a young woman. Tucker recognized her—his aunt, Cora Sue Kingsley. The image of her nearly took his breath away. He'd grown up seeing pictures of her, but was now at an age to really appreciate her natural beauty. She looked to be in her twenties when the photo was taken. Short, dark hair that had a little flip just above her ears. But her eyes were her most captivating feature. Big, and almond shaped. Sadness swarmed Tucker. She'd been young when she died, never married or had children.

How was it possible that a woman as beautiful as Cora hadn't had men begging her to marry them on a daily basis?

Next to the photo was her obituary. Nothing revealing there—the standard "died unexpectedly" listed as the cause of death at such a young age. Suicide was a word that was murmured and not spoken of, especially in a small town.

On the page, the headline stated: *Local Woman Falls To Her Death*.

Tucker got up and moved over to the couch where Lansing was going through a stack of papers. "Look what I found," he said as he slid the album partly onto her lap. "This might help with your research."

"What is it?" She turned her attention to the album and gazed at Cora Sue's picture. "Oh, she's stunning, like a young Audrey Hepburn."

"The article on the next page talks about her death."

The room was silent as they both read the article.

Police were summoned to Silent Cove yesterday afternoon upon receiving an anonymous call regarding a body seen floating in the cove at the edge of the estate. The young woman has been identified as Cora Sue Kingsley. According to Ms. Kingsley's brother, Walter, with whom she resided at the time of her death, Cora Sue was visiting the estate to lay a wreath as a memorial to her late aunt. Agatha Cambridge died on April 1, 1947, after falling to her death.

Friends of Cora Sue Kingsley stated that she had been depressed of late, and was obsessed with the death of her aunt. As the anniversary of Agatha's death approached, Cora became more distraught over the incident, oftentimes telling friends that she had seen a little boy who had told her how her aunt had been killed. Cora Sue was confident that her aunt had been murdered, even going so far as requesting the police reopen the investigation. Police reports state Ms.

Kingsley was convinced the little boy who was visiting her had confessed to the murder. Mr. Walter Kingsley assured police that there was no child residing or visiting them, and feared his sister was imagining things.

"Well, that would match what Sylvia told me," Lansing said.

Years earlier, police determined there was no foul play in the death of Agatha Cambridge and the case was closed. Many will recall the Silent Cove estate is no stranger to death. Maurice Cambridge and friend of the family, Eliza McGillicuddy, were killed when Delilah Cambridge shot them both during a New Year's Eve party being hosted by Ms. McGillicuddy. At the time, Ms. McGillicuddy resided at the estate. Mrs. Cambridge was the wife of Maurice Cambridge, and the couple had three children. Unfortunately, the same night, Mrs. Cambridge's father, William McAdoo passed from a sudden heart attack while attending the party with his daughter.

Tucker whistled. "Wow, that is some reworking of the facts."

"They certainly did sugarcoat the events. Makes me wonder what really happened to Cora Sue?"

Police have determined that Cora Sue Kingsley succumbed to the same fate as her aunt, Agatha Cambridge. The two died forty-four years apart, to the day. Funeral arrangements are pending.

Tucker closed the album and slid in onto the coffee table. "If they were willing to cover up the truth behind the New Year's Eve murders, it's plausible they've done the same with Agatha and Cora Sue's deaths, as well. Unfortunately, we may never know the truth."

Lansing nodded. "So, were you serious about keeping this place?" She asked, facing him.

He placed his arm along the back of the couch, his hand brushing against her shoulder. "I'm not sure. I admit the idea is growing on me." He stared at her. She had gorgeous eyes, which had a dreamy quality to them at that moment. "Would you come up here if I did?"

She tilted her head to the side and stared at him for a moment. "If you invited me, I wouldn't mind spending time here in Chistine."

"In Chistine?" A lock of her hair fell against his hand. He loosely twisted it through his fingers. "Or with me?"

"Both," she said, a sexy little grin played across her lips.

"Have I told you how grateful I am for all your help?"

"In a manner of speaking."

"What manner would that be?"

"Well, you've bought me lunch, and indulged my desire to dig into your family history without knowing what will be uncovered…"

"I'm not sure that really properly conveys how grateful I am that I met you."

Her eyes sparkled with mischief. "Well, what would?"

He leaned closer, his lips brushing against hers like a feather in the breeze. "This," he whispered before pressing his lips to hers.

She stilled for a moment, and Tucker worried that he'd misread her body language. She relaxed, and pressed her lips harder against his.

His hand caressed the side of her face as he slipped his tongue inside her mouth and explored. He was spellbound by her. His free hand slid up the side of her thigh and rested on the curve of her hip. She sighed into his mouth, lifted her leg, and placed it across his lap. Running his hand to the small of her back, he encouraged her to move closer. He needed to feel the heat of her body. The last thing he wanted was any space between them.

The sultriness of their kiss coursed through him, bringing everything below his belt to life. His erection strained against the zipper of his jeans, and he had to shift slightly to relieve the almost unbearable pressure.

With her hands splayed against his chest, Lansing pushed his back against the couch, and straddled his lap. The brief separation of their bodies provided a whiff of her arousal. Tucker dug his fingers into her ass cheeks, eliciting a deep, gratifying moan from her. She thrust her tongue deeper in his mouth, sending electric currents through his body. He was pretty damn sure Lansing could cause him to explode with this one deeply erotic kiss, fucking his mouth with her tongue.

He pulled his head back, his lips pressed against the side of her neck, and along her jaw. He needed a breather before he spewed in his pants like a horny teenager. Lansing tipped her head to the side, granting him easy access to the soft, sensitive skin at the base of her neck and along her shoulder. She panted softly, and grasped his shoulders as if she was afraid to let go.

A loud crash echoed through the house.

Lansing jerked her head around. "What was that?"

The sound had come from the kitchen, but Tucker

was unable to see anything from where they were sitting. "I don't know. It sounded like dishes breaking."

She slid off his lap, and he might have been embarrassed by the obvious boner he was sporting, except that she was still fixated on the hallway to the kitchen. He stood, and attempted to adjust his junk discreetly before stepping toward the hallway. "Stay here," he said without looking back at her. "I'll check it out."

Lansing made no motion to go with him, and for some reason, Tucker felt gratified by that. He was all about woman being as strong as men—even believed women were mentally able to handle a hell of a lot more crap than men—but Tucker was physically bigger and stronger than Lansing. The last thing he needed was to confront someone trying to pillage his uncle's home while she was hanging on his back.

He had a caveman need to protect her and keep her safe. She was his—at least for the time being—and he wasn't about to allow her to be harmed.

Shards of broken dishes littered the kitchen floor. The back door to the porch screeched and then slammed shut. Tucker peered through the screen. A young boy stared at him. Tucker inhaled sharply. The boy's pale face and dark, deep set eyes glared at him. A grim fixed expression on his sallow face sent a shiver that traversed the entirety of Tucker's spine. An arctic blast suddenly engulfed the room. Tucker was frozen in place.

"Hey, what are you doing here?" He asked.

The boy turned and walked away without a word. Tucker ran to the door and burst onto the porch. The child was nowhere in sight. Taking the steps two at a time, Tucker jogged around the corner of the house and scanned the yard. At the back, nearly camouflaged by the trees stood the macabre boy.

"Hey, you little shit," Tucker yelled. "You get your ass back here and clean up this mess."

The boy stood stock still. He showed no evidence he was worried about getting in trouble.

Tucker set out across the yard toward the trees. "Where do you live? We'll see how your parents feel about you coming into my home and destroying my property."

If he could get within arms length of the little terror, he could drag his ass back to the kitchen. But when he reached the spot where the boy had been standing, the boy was nowhere to be found. A faint mist dissipated around Tucker's ankles.

"Where the hell are you?" He peered into the trees, hoping to catch a glimpse of movement. "How the hell did he get away so quickly?"

Tucker turned back toward the house. Lansing stood at the corner, her arms wrapped across her chest. He raised his hands in the air over his head and started toward her.

"Who was it?" she asked as he got closer.

He shrugged. "Don't know, some kid."

"What did he look like?"

"Young boy—I'd guess about ten years old—wearing black shorts and a white shirt. He must not get out in the sun much, because he looked sickly."

Lansing grasped his arm. "Sounds like the boy I saw the other day."

"Well, he'd be wise to stay away. If I catch him around here again, I'll call the cops on his destructive ass."

Lansing chuckled. "Come on, He-Man. We have a mess to clean up."

Tucker wasn't really all that upset about the broken dishes. They were old and ugly and probably headed for the nearest Salvation Army. He was livid his intimate moment with Lansing had been rudely interrupted. He may not have wanted to get to home plate on his uncle's dusty couch, but he wouldn't have minded hanging out on second, or even stealing third. Looked like their game was going to be called for bad timing by a trespassing little turd.

Lansing pulled a broom and dustpan from the cleaning cabinet and started sweeping up the mess. It didn't appear there was any way they would be getting back to where they had been—or where things were going—anytime soon, if at all.

And that thought depressed the hell out of Tucker. An aching need sat like a boulder in the center of his chest.

This trip was sure to be one of the best times of his life, but he could sense a dark cloud of regret at the end of the journey.

12

Lansing and Tucker made quick work of cleaning up the kitchen. They returned to the family room and resumed the task of going through Walter's personal items. The mood was tense and awkward after the impromptu make out session that ended too soon. Tucker must've felt the same weirdness because after a few minutes he suggested they gather up their things and head back to the inn. Lansing was a little trepidatious about where their relationship—if you could even call it that—stood. Was Tucker regretting what had transpired between them? Did he want to continue along this path of intimacy that erupted between them like a volcano?

God, she hoped so. They shared the single best kiss of her life. Not that she was really all that experienced. She hadn't had many lovers, but no one had ever made her toes curl. And she had never, ever wanted to throw caution to the wind and give into sexual desires on a whim before. She was sensible—not slutty. She believed in having a meaningful relationship before having intercourse with a man, not putting out on the first date.

And, if she was going to be technical about it, it wasn't even a date.

"So, about earlier," Tucker said.

Butterflies skittered through her stomach. Did she want to talk about this? She hadn't even fully considered how she was feeling—although she was pretty sure she wanted to revisit what they had already done, and add in a few more extra curricular activities.

Christ, Lansing, talk about getting whiplash from change in positions. She was all over the map. What did she want from Tucker? And what was she willing to accept?

"Uh-huh," she answered.

"I'm trying to figure out how two of my relatives could have fallen to their deaths in the exact same spot."

Well that certainly puts things in perspective.

"It does seem to be more than just a coincidence," she said. Disappointment sat like a yoke on her shoulders. "Especially given the history of the property."

"I want to see the bluff. Get a sense of where…and how…I just can't seem to wrap my head around it. Maybe if I see the area, I'll be able to understand how it could've happened. Why weren't the deaths investigated more thoroughly?"

She plastered a smile on her face hoping it masked her disillusionment. "When are you planning on going out there?"

"I thought we could go when we returned to the inn, if you're willing to make the trek out there with me?"

"Of course." Her voice raised a pitch or two higher

than usual. She prayed he wasn't able to see how her cheeks had flamed.

That pretty much answered her question regarding how Tucker felt about them kissing. He didn't appear to even remember it happened, which told Lansing she had placed a higher degree of importance on the event than she had. Regret and sadness hit her like a slushy snowball, stinging as it sluiced across her skin. Leaving her chilled to the bone.

She quickly gathered her things and followed Tucker to the door. The ride to the inn entailed Tucker mulling over Agatha's and Cora's deaths while Lansing sat quietly and nodded.

Tucker parked the car and turned to her. "Are you okay?"

"Of course." She tamped down the sudden urge to burst into tears.

For goodness sake, pull yourself together. You're a grown woman.

"Okay," he said, narrowing his eyes. "You were awfully quiet on the drive."

"I was just listening, and trying to come up with answers...not very successfully," she lied. She opened the door and got out before he could question her further. She wasn't ready to deal with the possibility that Tucker was going to give her the "I'm not really looking for a relationship right now—can we be friends?" discussion. She was already far beyond embarrassed by her wantonness in the face of his aloofness. There was no reason to belabor the point. He was obviously not interested in her in the way she had hoped he would be. And certainly not to the extent she had allowed herself to fall for him.

Tucker maintained a brisk pace through the garden and down the trail leading into the forest. At the fork, they followed the arrow to the bluff. She stood beside Tucker and peered over the side. Rocks jutted through an angry swirl of white-capped water. A fall would be disastrous.

"I wonder why there are no memorial markers for Agatha and Cora?" Lansing asked as she walked around the clearing.

"Bad luck," a deep male voice said behind her. She twirled around. William stepped out of the forest. He nodded at her, but seemed far more interested in Tucker. "Bad things happen up here when the dead are remembered."

"You mean Cora Sue?" Tucker asked.

"Yes." His eyes were vacant as if he were recalling a memory.

"Do you know what happened to her?" Lansing asked, joining the men closer to the cliff.

"She fell over the edge." William pointed to the cliff.

No shit, that much we know. Why was he being so obtuse?

"There was speculation about how she actually went over the edge," Tucker responded. "Do you know what happened that day? Was she pushed or did she just slip and fall?"

"I don't know for sure," William said, but his head dropped and he seemed suddenly interested in moving the dirt around with his boot.

Tucker exhaled loudly through his nose. "But you have an idea?"

"Yes. I'm sure that she was pushed."

"By who?" Lansing asked.

He stared at her for a moment before slowly shaking his head. "Can't say for sure."

No one spoke for what seemed an eternity. Lansing would bet her right arm the old man knew more than he was saying. They waited for him to elaborate on his statement, but he remained close-mouthed.

"What about Agatha?" Tucker asked, rage flickering in his eyes. Obviously he had had enough of William's obstinance, as well. "Did she commit suicide or was she also pushed?"

William shrugged and looked out over the water. "Perhaps both."

William's piecemeal answers were wearing Lansing's nerves pretty thin.

"How do you mean—both?" Lansing asked, her voice level and calm. No good would come from confronting him with the anger that was building in her.

William paused and looked out over the water. "Something haunted Agatha for most of her life. I suppose that's what pushed her to take her life."

Nice play on words. Lansing wasn't buying that was the whole story.

"Need to get back to work. Chores to do," he muttered, and walked away.

After the old man was out of sight, Tucker glanced at Lansing. "What do you think?"

"I think he knows exactly what happened to Agatha and Cora."

"I get that feeling, too." Tucker pulled his hand down over his face and exhaled. "But why not just tell us what happened? It's not like anyone can get into trouble for murdering Agatha and Cora—they're probably long dead, by now."

"If it was the same person that killed both women."

Tucker took a hold of Lansing's hand and they strolled down the trail. The heat that radiated through her both excited and relaxed her. But she knew she shouldn't read more into than was meant. He was struggling with accepting his family was made up of the living, the dead, and the in-between, and trying to discover the truth behind it all. Romantic affection was not part of the equation. He was interested in friendship—and most likely, only while they were both at Silent Cove.

"Seems a bit odd that someone would murder Agatha, and a completely different person would murder Cora—in the exact same spot," he said. "Besides, why would anyone want to murder either of them? By all accounts, they led normal lives, even if you consider the mental issues Agatha faced."

"I don't know." Lansing glanced around expecting to see William pop out of the woods again. The way he would appear and vanish was creeping her out.

Tucker's jaw clenched. "William knows, and I'm going to get it out of him--one way or another."

They rounded the bend and halted in their tracks. The figure of a woman stood in front of the grave stone under the giant tree.

"Eliza?" Lansing called, her voice soft so as not to come across as threatening.

The woman turned her head, but didn't speak.

Tucker tightened his grip on Lansing's hand and she had to bite her tongue to keep from yelping.

Eliza's gaze darkened as she zeroed in on Tucker. "You have no right to be here. No Cambridge should ever be allowed anywhere near this tree."

"Why?" Lansing asked. "Who is buried here?"

Eliza's eyes widened. Something sinister flickered in her gaze. She lifted a bony finger. "Ask him."

The hairs on the nape of Lansing's neck stood on end. Her heart pounded in her ears. She glanced at Tucker, not sure she wanted to find out what was behind them.

Slowly, she turned her. William stood a few feet away. *How had she not sensed him?*

Light barely broke through the thick canopy of the forest. A few streaks of sunlight crossed William's face, like a scar from a vicious knife attack.

"Do not speak to them, Eliza." William's voice was low, gravelly, and eerily commanding. He took a menacing step toward Eliza, a grim line frozen in place where his mouth should've been. "You have hurt enough members of my family."

"And your family got their revenge," she spat at him. "Mark my words, this is not over. Everyone needs to pay for what they've done."

William roared. The deep, guttural sound reverberated through the trees like a bear protecting it's young. Eliza took a wobbly step backward and disappeared into the forest.

The air around her was suddenly heavy with fear. Lansing struggled to pull a breath into her lungs. A part of her—a fairly large part—wanted to follow Eliza's lead and run away. But terror paralyzed her. She had never seen William so enraged. He was typically so docile.

"What did she mean by everyone needs to pay?" Lansing asked Tucker.

"I don't know, and once again William disappeared when Eliza left." Frown lines creased his forehead. "I think we need to visit Charles and Penelope tomorrow, and see if they have any answers."

Lansing agreed, but could only nod. Her ears were still ringing from William's bellow, and Eliza's declaration. She hoped making the trip to Middleton would provide clarity, but feared they would be more in the dark than they were.

13

Lansing descended the stairs into the lobby. Tucker's gaze roamed up and down her body. Her blood pressure spiked as he took her in. She had a great body. The kind that made a guys mouth water wondering what was hidden under the layer of clothing. Which was exactly what Tucker was interesting in—what lie beneath the simple sundress she wore.

Lansing glanced down at her dress, and smoothed her hand over the skirt. "I thought since we're going to see Penelope I should dress up a bit. Maybe she'll be more forthcoming if she views me as a decent, respectable woman."

"You sure are placing a lot of hopes on that little dress," he said and winked at her.

She smacked his arm. "You're a funny guy."

"That's sarcasm, right?" Tucker smirked. "My sense of humor isn't as finely tuned as yours."

She rolled her eyes, and looped her arm through his. "Let's go."

Once in the rental car, Lansing plugged in Charles's address into the GPS. Tucker pulled out onto the highway and headed out of town. "Still think this is a good idea?" He asked.

"I do. I mean, if Walter left Charles something in his will, as the executor of the estate you need to find him and make sure he receives the bequest, right?"

"Yeah, and it'd be nice to learn more about my family history," Tucker added. "My father rarely discusses any of them, so I grew up only truly knowing my mother's family."

"Didn't you ever wonder about your 'other' family—especially since you suddenly stopped visiting them?"

He briefly thought of providing *of course not, young dude's don't care about that shit* as an explanation, but decided against being that brutally honest. He was pretty sure he was already coming off as a bit of an uncaring dick when it came to his father's family. "Not really. I was young, and had more important things on my mind—friends, girls, sports. When I graduated from college and started working, I was too absorbed in my career and my own life to really care about any family members besides my parents."

Lansing smiled, but shook her head. "My childhood was so different. We spent every weekend with grandparents and cousins. Everyone lived within the same neighborhood in Boston, separated by a city block or two. I'm one of the few that left the neighborhood to go to college, and the only one who hasn't returned—a fact my parents and grandparents often remind me of when I visit." She sighed. "I loved growing up in a tight-knit family. But also loved having some distance from all of them to create a life of my own without every decision being up for debate and discussion from everyone I'm was related to. Anonymity had its perks."

Tucker couldn't really relate. His mother's family

had been close, but they also kept their distance. And no one would presume to question another family member's decisions—at least not directly to them. They were all very adept at smiling in agreement but then talking behind each other's backs. They weren't bad people, they just didn't presume to be another other than a sounding board for each other, and would never insert themselves into private, family matters.

What would it have been like to be in Lansing's family growing up, with everyone in everyone else's business? Probably much like it had been for Tucker's father growing up in Chistine. Except that there had been the added benefit of everyone in town knowing his business, not just family.

An hour later, they pulled up to a small 1930's Cape Cod style home.

"Wonder if they're home?" Tucker asked, peering around Lansing to see the house. It was impossible to tell if anyone was inside. They had decided not to contact Charles or Penelope regarding their visit. Penelope had apparently gone to great lengths to make everyone in Chistine believe Charles was dead. And maybe he was, but then why hadn't Lansing's search turned up a death certificate, obituary, or any other sort of death notice?

"Only one way to find out."

Without thinking, Tucker took Lansing by the hand and led her down the narrow cement walkway to the porch. It was crazy how natural it seemed to hold hands with her. He had given that up after high school. Now, he couldn't imagine being this close to Lansing and not touching her in some small way.

When had that become so important to him?

She didn't pull away, or act as if she was uncomfortable, so he focused on the main reason they had come to town. Pushing the doorbell, he listened for any movement inside the house. The door opened, and a small, elderly woman stood in the doorway.

"Hi, my name is Tucker, and this is Lansing. I'm looking for Penelope Cambridge."

Her bony hand went to the strand of pearls at her neck. "I'm Penelope Cambridge." Her voice was soft and sweet.

"Are you married to Charles Cambridge?" Lansing asked.

"Yes." She swallowed, and a flush swept up her neck. "What's this about?"

"Mrs. Cambridge, I'm Beaulah's grandson." Tucker glanced at Lansing who smiled and gave him a little head nod of encouragement. "Would it be possible to come in and talk to you for a few minutes? I promise we won't take up much of your time."

Penelope stared at Tucker for a moment. "Your Robert's boy?"

"Yes, ma'am."

All traces of her smile evaporated. She gave a small nod and stepped away from the door. Gesturing to a couch in the living room, she sat in a chair perpendicular to them. Her demeanor had cooled about ten degrees since he introduced himself. "How is your father?"

"He's well, thank you. He and my mother are on a trip, at the moment."

"So, I'm guessing that's why you're here and not him?"

"Partly, yes." Tucker took a steadying breath. "I assume you've heard my father's brother, Walter, passed away recently?"

"Yes, I'd heard. What does that have to do with me?"

"Walter left a few things for your husband. Duncan

Shakely was led to believe that Charles had passed away. Is that true?"

"There is no more Charles," she snapped. "Whatever Walter left him, you can keep, or throw away—I don't care. But I do not want any part of that family or anything they have left behind."

Penelope's demeanor had gone from kindly to cold to downright freezing since they had entered the home. Tucker wasn't sure they would get much more information out of the woman.

"Mrs. Cambridge, Tucker is also trying to learn more about his father's family. I know this may be a difficult topic, but we heard Charles' sister, Agatha, had some mental problems that may have contributed to her death. Can you tell us anything you remember about her—or her death?" Lansing asked.

"Don't you dare speak of that devil in this house," Penelope yelled. Tucker's back stiffened. He glanced at Lansing, whose eyes were as round as Frisbees.

"She was the cause of all of the heartache we endured. From the very start of our marriage, she would talk of being cursed--that Charles was a bad person, and that his past would come back for him. She told me I would never have children. It haunted me—even after we left that town—and every time I would get pregnant, I would fret about being cursed. The doctors said I was worrying so much I was causing the miscarriages." Tears filled the woman's eyes and slid down her wrinkly cheeks. She reached over to a tissue box on the small table beside her, and wiped her face.

"I'm so sorry—" Lansing said.

The woman wagged a bony finger at Lansing. "Not another word. Now, I would like you both to leave my house." She rose from her seat and walked toward the kitchen. "You can show yourselves out."

Tucker opened his mouth to ask her why she hated them so much, or tell her she didn't have a right to hold a woman with obvious mental issues at fault for her actions, but Lansing grabbed a hold of his wrist. She shook her head, stood, and walked toward the front door.

Tucker followed her to the car. "I'm not sure we gave that enough of a shot. Don't you think we should've asked her a few more questions?"

"She asked us to leave, Tucker. Do you think she'd hesitate to call the police on us? She was obviously distraught."

He exhaled and closed his eyes. They were no closer to finding Charles—or answers—than when they had arrived. "But we didn't learn anything."

"I disagree." Lansing pulled her cell phone out of her purse. Tucker watched as she opened the Google app, waiting for her to elaborate. From where he was sitting, they only confirmed what they already knew—Penelope had a serious hate for her in-laws.

"When you mentioned that everyone in Chistine believed Charles had passed away, she didn't confirm that he had died." She typed furiously into the search box.

"Yes, she did," Tucker argued.

"No, she said 'there is no more Charles'." Lansing smiled. "I think Charles is alive."

"Okay, so where is he?"

She held up her phone so he could see the screen.

Middleton Psychiatric Hospital.

"There is no more Charles," Tucker murmured. "What's the address?"

"Is there a patient named Charles Cambridge residing here?" Tucker asked the nurse sitting at the Middleton Psychiatric Hospital reception desk.

Peering over the top of her glasses, she quirked up an eyebrow as she assessed Tucker and Lansing. "Are you a family member?"

"Yes." Tucker pulled his driver's license from his wallet and showed it to her. "He's my great uncle. His nephew—my uncle—has recently passed away. Charles is listed as a beneficiary in the will. I'm the executor of the estate—."

"You need to talk to his wife," she said, cutting him off.

"We just came from Penelope's," Lansing said, a sweet smile on her face. Even in the short time Tucker had known her, he could tell it was as fake as the implication that Penelope had given them her blessing to speak to Charles. Tucker suppressed his urge to chuckle. She was an absolute godsend. Her ability to read a situation and people was invaluable.

Nurse Hatchett sighed and pointed at a clipboard on the counter. "Sign in." She handed them both a badge with Visitor stamped in bright red letters. "Wear these while you're here. Turn them back in before you leave." She pointed to a set of double doors to their left. "Down the hall. Mr. Cambridge is in the room at the end on the right."

"Thank you," Lansing said as Tucker signed them in and headed for the doors.

"Quick thinking dropping Penelope's name," he whispered as they headed down the long hall.

"Not my first time sneaking into a place," she answered. "Although, I hadn't expected this place to be as secure as Fort Knox."

When they reached the end of the hall, Tucker

double-checked the name on the door, rapt his knuckles against it a couple of times, and slowly pushed it open. An elderly man sat in a chair by the window. His thinning gray hair matched his gray slacks.

Tucker slowly walked toward the man. Charles hadn't moved at all since they had come in. A cold fear washed over him. Had Charles passed away in his chair without anyone realizing it? Tucker banished the morbid thought from his mind. Why did he always assume he was going to come upon a dead person when he visited a nursing home?

Tucker stood beside the man's chair. "Hello? Charles?"

Charles turned his head and smiled. His hand shook as he grasped Tuckers arm. "Thurman? Is that you?" He looked behind Tucker at Lansing. Somehow the grin on his face grew even broader and brighter. "And you brought my sister. How wonderful."

Tucker swung his gaze to Lansing. Apparently Charles was suffering from dementia or Alzheimer's, and believed his sister, Beaulah, and her husband were still alive. And young.

"No, I'm Tucker, Beaulah's grandson." He gestured toward Lansing. "And this is my friend, Lansing."

"Oh, I see," Charles said, but his eyebrows were drawn together so tight he looked as if he had a unibrow.

"Do you mind if we visit with you for a little while?" Lansing asked.

"No," he said, and gestured at the chair next to him. "Please, sit."

Lansing nodded at Tucker to take the chair. She sat on the edge of the bed between them.

They sat in silence for a moment. "I don't know

where Penelope has got off to," Charles muttered. His gaze swept around the room. "I think she's upset again."

Lansing tilted her head to the side. "Why is she upset?" Warmth flooded Tucker's chest. He was enamored by her ability to make people comfortable in chaotic and confusing situations. It was a talent he lacked. He, once again, thanked the heavens for her.

"Oh, you know how she gets, Beaulah." Charles lowered his voice and leaned closer to them. "Looks like we lost another baby. Seeing you upsets her. She thinks it's not fair that it's so easy for you to have children when all she wants is one of her own."

"I'm sorry," Lansing said, and gave Tucker a side eye glance. "Would it be easier if I left?"

"No, no." Charles reached across to pat her knee. "It's not often I get to see you, sister."

"Do you see Agatha at all?" Tucker asked. He shrugged at Lansing when she raised an eyebrow at his question.

The old man's eyes watered, and Tucker regretted bringing up his dead great aunt. Charles shook his head. "Not so much anymore since she passed."

What the hell did that mean?

"She came to visit you after she…fell off the cliff?" Lansing asked.

"Yes, she would warn me about the boy." Charles dropped his head to his chest.

The room was silent. Charles hadn't moved or made a sound for what seemed an eternity. Tucker and Lansing stared at one another.

Don't you dare die on me now, old man. Not when we are this close to figuring shit out.

"The boy?" Lansing broke the silence.

Charles raised his head and looked at Lansing. Both she and Tucker exhaled simultaneously.

"Does he haunt you, as well?" Charles asked, his voice meek. "I'm so sorry. I thought I was doing the right thing. I only wanted to protect us. Grandmother Zora was frightened of him."

"Of who?" Tucker asked. He tried to temper his excitement at the prospect of actually clearly some things up.

Charles shook his head in vehement protest. "I can't speak his name."

Gently, Lansing took both of the man's bony hands in hers. "When was the last time you saw him?"

"I see him every day—every night. He stands in the hallway and watches me." Charles tentatively glanced at the door. Tucker followed his gaze, wondering if the old man was crazy, or actually being visited by a creepy little kid.

"What does he say to you?"

"Nothing. There is nothing to say. I know what he wants. Agatha told me he would come for me—just as he had for her."

"What do you mean—come for you? For what?" The words flew from Tucker's mouth more harsh than he had intended.

"Revenge." Charles' words were slow and seared Tucker like a slow flame burning a path across his skin.

"Is he here now?" Lansing asked.

"No, but he'll be back." Tears ran in a steady stream through the wrinkled crevices in the man's face and dripped into his lap. "Oh, Beaulah, you don't know how happy I am you were spared. I didn't know making Agatha help me would hurt her so. I just didn't know…"

"What are you doing here?" A voice bellowed from behind them.

Penelope Cambridge stood in the doorway, no longer looking meek and mild. Fiery rage etched her features. She hurried to Charles's side, taking his face in her hands. "What have they done to you, my darling?"

14

The drive back to Chistine was as even more quiet than their departure earlier in the day. Definitely more subdued. After Penelope had regained her composure, she ordered Tucker and Lansing to leave. They stopped at a restaurant outside of town, and discussed the odd conversation they had with Charles before they were interrupted. But now, Lansing mulled over what had happened. No doubt Tucker was mentally trying to figure out who the boy was that Charles had been talking about—after all, that's what Lansing was doing.

When they pulled up to the inn, it was almost eleven o'clock at night. Only a couple of dimmed lights were on as they stepped into the foyer. There was just enough light to walk down the hall without bumping into furniture. At the end of the hall, a soft glow flickered from the ballroom. Lansing stilled. Music wafted through the air, barely loud enough to be heard.

"Do you hear that?" she asked, and walked toward the ballroom.

Tucker was close behind her. "Yeah, but I thought I was imagining it."

Lansing had seen the ballroom from the second floor balcony. A beautiful room from above, it was absolutely breathtaking standing in the center. Slowly, she twirled around. The music flowed, the light from the sconces flickered, and Lansing gave into the moment. Swaying to the melody, she closed her eyes and imagined what life was like when the house was first built. The parties, the ladies dressed in the finest fashions, the men in tuxedoes. Champagne flowing without end. Laughter and gaiety.

A hand rested on her hip, rotating her around. She gazed into Tucker's seductive eyes. He held his hand out to her. "Would you honor me with a dance, my lady?"

She giggled and slid her hand in his. "I would be delighted, sir." He pulled her body close and led her around the dance floor like he was a professional dancer. Lansing wouldn't have believed Tucker knew the first thing about dancing, especially a waltz.

But then, he had a way of surprising her at nearly every turn. Something no man had done in a very long time. She found most men predictable and boring in their attempts to be romantic and attentive. She longed for someone to break out of the box and do something unexpected—something swoon-worthy. Anything that would set him apart from the typical male. She was tired of feeling anything a guy did was part of a planned routine he had tried on every female.

Tucker's lips grazed her ear. His breath bathed her in passion, and sent delectable tickles down her spine to the pit of her belly.

"I feel as if I've been taking advantage of you while you're on vacation," he murmured, his voice husky yet sensuous. Goose bumps spread across her skin.

"How so?"

"All your free time has been spent going through old papers and pictures inside the dusty house of an old man you're not related to. Add on top of that, trying to piece together a puzzle based off the ramblings of a very old, rather senile man while being chastised by his overly protective wife." He nuzzled closer to her, his lips brushing the outer edge of her earlobe. "And you've had to endure being around me."

Desire coursed through her veins. "Yes, a fate worse than death." Her breathing turned to soft pants. Every nerve in her body was on heightened alert. She was anxious, excited, and a little nervous about where things were heading.

His hand slid from her hip to her lower back, his fingers splayed, and the tips pressed into her skin. "I feel very lucky to have met you, Dr. Abbott."

Holy mother of lust! She was so turned on by this man's words, and the simple yet erotic way he touched her. Her brain was heavy, her thoughts hazy, and all she could think about was how badly she wanted to be alone with him in her room. Or his. Hell, she didn't care—she wanted him. More than she had ever wanted a man in her life.

"Likewise, Mr. Kingsley. I'm not sure I could've imagined a more unexpected adventure than this. Or a more handsome man in need of my assistance."

"Trust me," he said, pulled his head back, brushing against her lips. "The pleasure has been all mine."

Lansing knew the kiss was coming, but the rush of excitement that exploded when his lips finally made contact with hers nearly knocked her on her ass. Thank goodness he had his arm wrapped tightly around her waist. It may have been the only thing that prevented her from sliding to the floor in a molten heap of erotic lava.

She sighed. *God, the man knows how to kiss.* Releasing her hand, he slid his fingers through her hair, his palm caressing the side of her face. She grasped him gently at the nape of his neck, opening her mouth, and allowing his tongue to slip and slide against hers.

Her head swam in a sea of desire, but—at the same time—was light as a feather swaying to the melody they were creating. This had to be the most romantic moment of her life. There didn't seem to be anything that could entice her to stop kissing him—

A glass shattered. She jerked her head back and gasped. Searching the room to locate shards of glass, Lansing couldn't see anything out of place.

Tucker raised an eyebrow, his gaze darting around the room. They stared at each for a moment. He shrugged, and leaned into her to resume their kiss.

Cold air rushed into the room, a windless tornado that enshrouded them. The skin on Lansing's arms prickled, and she shivered uncontrollably.

A woman stood behind Tucker. Lansing stared into hollow eyes, sinister and threatening. The woman took a long drag from her cigarette, the end glowing bright orange. Darkness shrouded her face, and an evil sneer spread across her white lips.

"Get out of my ballroom!"

Tucker whirled around. The vision dissipated like smoke.

"Did you hear that?" Lansing asked.

Had that been real?

Grasping Lansing's hand, Tucker strode toward the doors that led to the hallway. Without a word, he ascended the stairs, and stalked down the hallway to her door.

"Did you see her?" She asked.

"No, but I heard her loud and clear, and figured it

was best not to test her physical abilities." He exhaled and his shoulders dropped. Lifting her hand to his lips, he lightly kissed her knuckles. "Well, I'd say that ruined the moment."

"Yeah, nothing like an angry ghost to dampen the mood."

"Damn, ghosts," he muttered with a chuckle.

Lansing smiled, but wasn't sure what to do. Did he expect to be invited into her room? Did she want him to come in? She definitely wanted to kiss him for a while longer, and wasn't opposed to taking it farther. What if Tucker was just a horny guy and would regret sleeping with her the next morning? Would making love to him make things weird between them? She definitely didn't want that to happen. She was enjoying spending time with him, and wanted to see if their relationship could progress. If that meant not rushing into having sex, then perhaps waiting was the best course in the long run. Would he understand her decision to hold off? Or would he be upset that she had teased him?

"I should go," Tucker said. "It's been a long day, and we both could use a good night's sleep."

Lansing nodded, but her heart dropped with a thud. She knew he was right—it was exactly what she had planned to say to him—but that didn't stop her from wanting him to want things to go farther. Still, it was not the right time in their relationship for a romp in the sack—especially since they hadn't yet defined their relationship. Friends? More? Would sex just add the dreaded *with benefits* tag?

Could you be any more indecisive?

"See you in the morning for breakfast?" he asked, his voice low and soft.

She nodded. "Definitely."

"Maybe we'll be able to figure out who the little boy is that haunts Charles."

"And sent Agatha over the edge—literally."

"Good night, Lansing." He brushed a kiss across her cheek.

She swallowed hard as her belly fluttered with longing. "Good night, Tucker." She slipped into her room and closed the door before she did what she really wanted to do—throw caution to the wind, pull him inside, toss him on the bed and have her way with him. Closing her eyes, she envisioned naked Tucker completely under her control.

Jesus, Lansing, get a grip. She had never wanted to be dominant in a relationship—especially during sex. But Tucker was drawing out all sorts of hidden wants and desires, and she was game to try all sorts of new things. In and out of the bedroom.

She groaned, and flopped down on the bed.

This is going to be a long, lonely, sexually frustrating night.

LANSING WANDERED INTO THE KITCHEN, hoping she could make herself warm milk or tea—anything to relax her. Restless sleep had tormented her most of the night. She was impatient which prohibited her from drifting off to dreamland. She added water to the tea kettle and placed it on the burner to heat.

The garden was bathed in light from the moon high in the midnight sky. Lansing stepped outside and pulled her sweater tighter around her midsection. A shadow darted across the yard. The figure stopped and turned toward her. The boy she had seen at Walter's house lifted his arm over his head and gestured for her to follow.

What on earth is he doing out here in the middle of the night? Something must be wrong. Was someone hurt?

Her slippered feet crunched under the gravel path. At the edge of the forest, she glanced back at the inn. The outline of the mansion was barely visible. All was dark, quiet. Somewhat foreboding. The inn was asleep. Just like the residents inside, curled under plush comforters. Maybe she should go back and wake Tucker. Or the owners so they could contact the authorities? Even if no one was injured, there was a young boy out very late at night without adult supervision. The parents should be investigated for neglect, at the very least.

How had the boy managed to get here from Walter's neighborhood across town? Chistine was a small town, but it was still not safe for a youngster to be walking the streets this late at night on his own.

And why was she following him into the dark forest? Alone?

She had a decision to make. Behind her was the inn. Going forward meant entering the forest and leaving the protection of the moonlight. She peered down the path. The trees were dense. No light penetrated the canopy of branches. There wasn't even the song of crickets in the eerie quiet.

The boy stood on the path. Waiting. Watching. Silently demanding she follow him.

An inexplicable need to discover what the child wanted to show her propelled her forward. Some unfamiliar force was dictating her actions. For some reason, Lansing was not intimidated by the unknown awaiting her in the darkness.

Nothing ventured, nothing gained.

Barely able to see the boy in the darkness, she carefully walked along the twisting path. She lost sight of him at a bend, but once the trail straightened out, he was visible again. Motionless a few feet away from her, his gaze was fixed on the lonely grave beneath the grand oak tree.

He pointed at the stone marker. A cold cloak of death turned her skin to ice.

"Do you know who this grave belongs to?" Lansing whispered.

The boy lifted his gaze, his eyes dark, deep wells of sadness and pain. His head bobbed up and down.

Lansing swallowed over the lump lodged in her throat. "Is it you?"

He nodded again.

She inhaled sharply. "Can you tell me what happened to you?"

The boy pointed into the inky darkness of the forest. Lansing strained her eyes to see what he was pointing at, but there didn't appear to be anything there.

A blast of icy air smack Lansing face. Sharp pricks stung her cheek from the force of the impact.

"How dare you desecrate this spot." Eliza hovered in front of Lansing. A ghostly hand slapped her across the face.

Lansing screamed, and shuffled backward a few steps. Her heart was in her throat, and her limbs shook. The boy had disappeared. But Eliza remained. Dark, malevolent, and flaming with hatred.

"I-I'm sorry—" Lansing stammered. Squeaking caught her attention. She looked at the giant tree, in all it's dark, menacing glory.

A rope hung over one of the branches. Where did that come from? It hadn't been there before. She saw a noose. It was wrapped tightly around the boy's neck.

"Oh my god!" Her heart stopped. Bulging, haunted eyes stared at her.

Get out of here! Get back to the Inn!

Tucker. She had to get to him.

He would protect her from Eliza. From the boy. From what she had seen.

Eliza flew toward her, arms outstretched.

"They did this!" Eliza yelled. She wrapped her hands around Lansing's throat and squeezed. "They are to blame!"

Lansing clawed at the woman, desperate to get free of the deathly grip. But it was as if she was fighting against the air.

Eliza applied more pressure. Lansing's airway slowly closed. She gasped for breath. Panic washed over her. All coherent thought ceased. She crumpled to the ground.

"Please...it wasn't me." Lansing's plea was barely above a whisper.

Eliza hovered above her, face twisted, distorted with rage. "Someone must pay."

Blackness edged Lansing's peripheral vision. She was slipping into darkness. The little bit of light illuminating Eliza grew dim. The air around them dissipated like the morning haze. Except there was no sun.

No hope for a new dawn.

Lansing was going to die for the sins of others. And she had no idea what the sins were...or who had committed them.

The face of the handsome man who had come into her life like a bright ray of sunshine flashed before her. Tucker. Her final thought was of him. Her final regret. She had found the perfect man but would never fall in love with him. Never have her happily ever after—

something she hadn't believed in but now wanted desperately.

The cruel irony was that she had come to Chistine to uncover paranormal secrets.

Secrets now taking her life.

"Lansing!"

She jerked her head and opened her eyes, quickly shutting them against the bright light. Dragging in a deep breath, she coughed with the introduction of oxygen to her system again.

Opening her eyes to mere slits, she waited as they adjusted to the light. Someone was sitting on the bed in front of her. She focused on the figure until her vision cleared.

Tucker.

Warmth and happiness flooded her chest. He was so handsome. So sexy. Everything she wanted—

His eyes were wide. His lips were moving. He grasped her shoulders.

"Eliza." Frantically, she searched the room for the crazy ass ghost woman.

Tucker looked straight into her eyes. "She's not here. Just me."

Lansing swallowed, wincing in pain. Had she breathed in shards of glass that were imbedded in her throat? Pain flared as she touched the area where Eliza's hands had choked her.

"She tried to kill me."

Deep lines creased Tucker's forehead. "You were having a nightmare."

"I was by the tree. I saw the boy." She grasped Tucker's arms. "Eliza was there. She was choking me."

Tucker shook his head. "You were not in the forest, Lansing. You're in your bed. It was just a nightmare."

"It was so real," she murmured. *Had she really dreamt everything?*

Tucker pulled her hands from her neck and sucked in his breath. "What the hell?"

"What?"

"You have red marks around your throat."

"I told you," she coughed out, struggling to speak. "She was choking me."

"Why?"

"I don't know. The boy led me to the tree. I asked him what happened, but then Eliza was there. She was angry, thought I was blaming the boy for his death. She attacked me."

"That's not possible, Lansing. I found you here—in your bed—not outside in the forest." Tucker let out a deep, weighted sigh.

"But I swear to you, I couldn't sleep. I got up and saw the boy, and followed him to the forest." Emotion choked her. Tears flooded her eyes.

He doesn't believe me.

"I was there, at the tree. The boy was hanging from a noose. Eliza appeared out of nowhere and was so angry at me."

Tucker placed his hand at the back of her head, and pulled her into his chest. "Shhh, we'll get to the bottom of this. I promise." He laid her back so her head rest gently on the pillow. "The best thing for you to do is get some rest."

He stood, but Lansing grabbed his hand. "Please don't leave me."

"I'm just going to get a warm towel to put on your neck. I'll be right back."

Lansing stared at the door as he left, unable to look

away in case someone other than him returned. When he stepped back inside and closed the door behind him, she exhaled in relief. He laid the towel across her neck, lifted her hand to his lips, and placed soothing kisses across the back.

"Will you stay with me?" she asked, her voice barely above a whisper. She hated feeling so weak and powerless, but knew she wouldn't live through another round in a ghost battle.

"Of course." Tucker walked to the opposite side of the bed, and slid under the covers. She rested her head on his bare chest, and drifted off to sleep to the constant rhythm of his beating heart.

15

Tucker slid out of bed, and quickly covered Lansing with the comforter. She'd slept, but it'd been fitful. Tucker was glad she asked him to stay. There would've been no way for him to sleep in his own room worrying whether she would be attacked again.

He padded down the hallway to his room. A quick shower and a change of clothes. The answers to what was happening—or had happened in the past—must be in the remaining papers and documents at Walter's home. He needed to finish cleaning the place and figure out what to do with it.

How much of what was happening was all just coincidence, though? He tried hard to wrap his head around how easily it was for him to throw logic out the window and believe mishaps were the fault of ghosts gone mad. But there could be other reasons, right? What had gone on in Charles and Agatha's childhood that had caused them to be haunted throughout their adult lives? And how had Grandma Beaulah been spared, as Charles put it?

Maybe the truth was that Charles and Agatha both

suffered from mental illness. Beaulah may not have been spared from being cursed by an evil boy, but from the psychotic break with reality Charles and Agatha had been hampered by.

The most disturbing part was the nightmare come to life Lansing had endured. Was there some type of madman lurking around the property? Had he come inside and tried to hurt Lansing, and in her deep sleep she incorporated her dream into the incident? But why would someone do that? Lansing wasn't from this area. She knew no one. Why would anyone want to harm her? Or try to kill her?

There was always the possibility that Lansing was not who she claimed to be. After all, Tucker didn't know her. He assumed she was telling the truth about who she was, where she was from, and why she was in Chistine. What if that was not the case?

He glanced at his watch. Still too early to go downstairs for breakfast. He planned on getting a tray from the kitchen to take to Lansing, but instead he sat at the small writing desk in his room and booted up his laptop. The time had come to make sure he knew the woman he had just spent the night with. He pulled up Plymouth University's website where she said she taught, and found the faculty listing. A black and white picture of a professional-looking Lansing filled half the screen, her bio next to it:

Dr. Lansing Abbott teaches primarily early American history that focuses on the very first colonial settlements through the Revolutionary War and establishment of the United States and implementation of the Constitution. Graduating from Dartmouth with a BA in American Studies, she received her PhD from Yale. She previously taught at Washington College (Maryland) and Michigan State University before becoming the Assistant Chair of the

History department at Plymouth University. She is a bestselling author of several books that center around the history of New England, including Hanton: The City of Ruins, *and* Traversing Vermont's Stone Chambers. *Her most recent release,* The Burnt Bodies; Revisiting Salem, *has been on the New York Times Bestseller list for two months. Her article in the* Journal of American History, Facing Fears Through Folklore: How climactic changes in a new land gave birth to myths and legends in New England, *has received high praise from historical experts worldwide. Dr. Abbott is currently on sabbatical.*

Tucker closed the lid of his laptop. A wave of relief coursed through him. He hated that he'd doubted who Lansing really was. He was developing feelings for her, and to find out she was lying to him would have crushed him. He was at an age where he should be settling down. A week ago, if anyone would have suggested that, he would have laughed at them and told them to go fuck themselves—he was having too much fun being single and rich to settle down with one woman. But here he was, letting his mind roam through possibilities of one woman, a shared life. A home. And he didn't want to open a vein at the idea. When he thought about spending days and nights with Lansing, it actually made him...happy.

The dining room only had one other couple in it when Tucker entered and sat down.

"Good morning," Carmen greeted him with a pot of coffee. "Will Lansing be joining you?"

"No, she's not feeling well. I was hoping I could take a tray of food up to her after I'm done eating."

"Of course, but I'll take it up, if you'd like."

"I want to check on her before I head out this morning, so it won't be a problem for me to take it up."

"Okay, well, I hope it's nothing serious. Does she

need to be seen by a doctor?" She asked, and filled his coffee cup.

"No, it's nothing that serious," Tucker said. *Just one of your ghosts that snuck into her dream and tried to strangle her...*"I'm pretty sure it's just a migraine, but she didn't get much sleep last night."

Carmen nodded. "Let her know that if she needs anything while you are gone, she can ring the front desk and I'll be happy to help in any way I can."

Tucker quickly ate breakfast. The breakfast tray was waiting for him when he was done. He walked up the stairs, knocked on Lansing's door and gently nudged it open. She lifted her head from the pillow and glanced at him through one open eye before lowering her head again.

He slid the tray onto the table by the window that looked out over the garden. "I come bearing gifts."

"If there's not coffee on that tray, you've failed."

Chuckling, he grasped the handle of the coffee cup and placed it on the bedside table. "Your coffee, oh ye of little faith."

Pushing her hair from in front of her face, she sat up and rested against the headboard. "You're the best man —ever—in the history of the world. And I know my history." She sipped the coffee and sighed.

"Wow, what would I have been if I had brought you an entire pot?"

"God."

He brushed her hair to the side to get a better look at her neck. The marks were turning bluish purple.

"How do they look?" she asked.

"Not bad. How do they feel?"

"Sore, but nothing like they did last night. I was sort of hoping it had all been a nightmare and I would wake up without a mark on me."

"No such luck, I'm afraid."

She caught his hand as he took it away from her neck, and squeezed it. "Thanks for staying with me last night. It couldn't have been a great night's sleep for you."

"It was fine, and you're welcome." He lifted her hand to his lips and watched a smile slide across her face. "I'm going to let you eat and then get some more rest."

"Where are you going?"

"Over to Walter's house. I have some guys with a truck coming to pick up the living room and bedroom furniture and take it to a homeless shelter. And there's a woman coming by to clean the place. I thought the refrigerator could use a thorough cleaning. Figured I could get through some more of the papers in the family room while they're working."

Lansing twisted her fingers in her lap. "I have a favor to ask you."

"Sure," he said. "What's up?"

"I need to see the tree."

"No, you need to rest," Tucker corrected her. The last place in the world Tucker would've expected her to want to go was out into the forest.

Her eyes were pleading with him. His chest tightened. *Nothing good can come from this.* "Why? What can possibly be gained by going there?"

"I'm not sure I can explain it. After what happened last night—I just feel like I have to see it in the daylight." She exhaled and her shoulders slumped. "I guess I have to see with my own eyes there is not a boy hanging from that tree."

The muscles in Tucker's neck stiffened. *She cannot be serious?*

"It makes no sense, I realize that, but there is no way

I can relax until I know for sure." She squeezed his hand. "I promise to come back here and take it easy until you get back."

He held her gaze, his resolve quickly disappearing. "Okay, if you're sure you're up to it."

She nodded and wrapped her arms around his neck.

Damn this woman and her gorgeous green eyes that made him melt and assured he would give in to her every wish.

16

Going to the tree had seemed like a good idea back in the room, but the closer Lansing got to the bend in the trail, the less she wanted to see what was there. It was a double-edged sword—either she was crazy, and there would be nothing there, or her dream had been real. She knew in her head that the tree would be just as it had been every other time she had seen it, but in her heart, she wondered if some part of the dream had been true.

Rounding the bend, the tree came into view. No rope. No noose. No dead boy. Lansing released her breath and leaned into Tucker. He wrapped his arm around her shoulder and kissed the top of her head.

"Oh, excuse me," a familiar male voice said behind them.

William. How did he always manage to show up whenever she was at the tree?

"I didn't mean to interrupt you," he said, and tipped his hat.

"Wait!" Tucker's voice was clipped, and his muscles rippled with tension. "I have some questions for you, and don't you dare think about lying to me, or giving me half-assed answers."

William stopped but didn't turn look at them. "What do you want to know?"

"Who is buried under this tree?"

"No one is buried there—"

Lansing's chest tightened. She'd had just about enough of this man and his lies. "Eliza's convinced you know the truth."

"So am I. What aren't you telling us?" Tucker asked.

"There are things you should not know." William's bowed his head and his demeanor softened.

Tucker gritted his teeth. "How did the person buried under that tree die?"

"The best thing for you to do is to leave this town and never return," William said.

Even as he spoke, Lansing could see the pain in the old man's eyes. Tucker was his great, great grandson. No doubt the man wanted to see him as often as he could. Lansing felt sorry for the man. He was stuck between two worlds, not belonging to either one, and not able to truly exist. He could see his family, but couldn't touch them. *What a lonely existence, and all because he was unable to stop his daughter from her deadly plan.*

At the moment, however, Lansing was at her wit's end with the man.

"Bullshit," Tucker said. "I'm not a child. I don't need protecting. Tell me who is buried here."

"It was a long time ago…it doesn't concern you."

"William!"

Lansing jumped at Tucker's sharp tone.

"Stop stalling and tell me what went on here." Tucker drew in a deep breath. "Did you kill whoever is in this grave?"

William's mouth dropped open, and sadness flooded his eyes. "No—I swear. I wasn't here when the boy died." He glanced up at the tree and closed his eyes. "I came around the bend from the house and saw him. There was a rope around his neck and he was hanging from the tree."

All the air rushed from Lansing's lungs. Cold dread coursed through her veins, and her knees buckled. She *had* seen the small boy hanging from a tree. Tears stung her eyes. Her nightmare had been real.

What would make a child do such a thing?

Tucker's face paled. "Who was the boy?"

Lansing was sure he was struggling to grasp how she had dreamed of the boy's death.

"I don't know." William continued to stare at the tree as if he was reliving the moment and was stuck in the past.

"What did you do after you found him?" Lansing asked.

"I cut him down and buried him there." He pointed toward the rock at the base of the tree.

Lansing's breath caught in her chest. "You didn't call the police?"

William shook his head. "Didn't see any point in that."

"Why?" Tucker asked.

"Didn't want no one coming out and asking Viola and Marjorie questions. They'd been through enough, and people in town were cruel to them because they lived here. Wasn't no cause for people to spread rumors that they was killing little children out here."

Lansing could only stare at the old man.

"A strange boy you don't know hangs himself from a tree and you simply *take him down and bury him*?" Tucker's tone dripped with disdain.

"Didn't anyone ever come looking for a missing child?" Lansing asked.

"No, nobody came."

Chatter filtered through the trees. A young couple came around the bend from the direction of the cottage. They stopped abruptly when they caught sight of Tucker and Lansing standing in the middle of the trail.

"Sorry," the man said, directing the woman around them. Once the couple was out of sight, Lansing searched for William, but the man had taken the opportunity to disappear.

"Dammit," Tucker said.

Lansing squeezed his hand and gave him a reassuring smile. "He won't stay gone forever. He wants to see you. We'll find him again."

"I guess you're right, but why do I feel like we come away from these information gathering sessions with more questions than answers?"

He was right. It was like a Pandora's box—opening one box only led to another. When would they finally get to the one that held the answers?

"Let's get out of here." Tucker said, still holding her hand.

Lansing glanced once more over her shoulder at the stone marker under the tree. Who was the little boy buried there?

And what did Eliza have to do with all of this?

17

The movers made quick work of getting all the furniture out of the house. The only things that remained were the antique china hutch in the living room and the desk—mainly because it still had files and papers to go through. Besides, Tucker liked the desk, and once more he considered whether or not to keep the house as a vacation home. The idea was growing on him, despite the recent supernatural events. The house gave him a settled feeling whenever he imagined leaving the city for a weekend away.

Of course, his visions always included a certain history professor. There was no way of knowing if Lansing even wanted a relationship with him, let alone whether she would accompany him for the weekend on a regular and continuous basis—despite what she had said.

"The kitchen is cleaned." The cleaning lady's voice yanked him from his daydream. "Refrigerator is empty and I defrosted the freezer. I packed all the dishes into the boxes for you, and cleaned all the small appliances. They're on the table—so you can see what all there is."

She rocked back and forth on her heels and waited for him to reply—and pay her, no doubt.

"Thank you so much for all your help." He pulled his checkbook from his pocket. He gave her over the amount they had agreed upon, figuring she had done the extra work in hopes of getting extra pay. Not that it bothered him. Anything that allowed him to avoid additional work on the house was money well spent. Besides, he was paying her about a third of what he paid his housekeeper back in the city who never did anything extra, but still expected a nice Christmas bonus. He handed the woman the check and waited while she peered at the amount and smiled. "Once the house is empty, would you be willing to come back and do a thorough cleaning of it?"

"Oh, yes," she said, her voice almost giddy, which was a bit disconcerting on a woman in her late sixties. "Just let me know when you need me and I'll be here. Will you be selling the house?"

"I'm really not sure...I may hold onto it for a bit. It's been in my family for generations. It seems wrong to just get rid of it."

"Yes, William had it built for Zora Sue—but my daddy said it was also so William always had a home and a reason to return from the sea."

A door slammed. The walls shook. Glass shattered. Tucker walked toward the bathroom door and pushed it open. The mirror above the sink was shattered, shards of glass littered the tiled floor. A breeze blew the curtain hanging over the small bathroom window.

"Wind must have caught the door and forced it shut," the cleaning lady said, peering around him into the bathroom.

"Makes sense," Tucker said.

"Would you like me to clean up the mess?"

Tucker shook his head. "No, thank you. I can get it." Silence filled the space between them. Tucker smiled at the woman, not sure what else to say, and wishing she would leave. He wanted to wrap things up and get back to Silent Cove so he could check on Lansing.

"Well, I'll be going. Thank you, again," she said, scooted out of the room, and walked toward the entry. Tucker glanced out the front window and watched as she toddled down the sidewalk toward her home.

Sighing heavily, he dropped back into the desk chair and pulled out the last of the papers in the file drawer. A small corner of paper peeked out from under the back. Tucker reached inside and gently tugged on the paper. The wood on the back of the drawer shifted. *A false back.* He tugged the drawer out and set it on the floor between his feet. Working the paper free, he unfolded the yellowing, aged document.

A black and white photo fell into his lap. Tucker stared at the young woman in the picture. She looked to be several months pregnant, but Tucker couldn't tell if she was happy or not. She had the hint of a smile on her face, but her eyes drooped at the corners. He flipped it over to see if there was a name on the back. Blank. He looked closely at the woman's face. There was something familiar about it...

"Eliza," he murmured. "And child." Tucker didn't know all the history between his great grandparents and the pretty young mistress, but he certainly didn't recall hearing about a baby. As far as Tucker knew, the only children Maurice Cambridge had fathered were Grandma Beaulah, Agatha, and Charles.

"So what happened to your baby, Eliza?"

He examined the document in his hand, and nearly fell out of his chair. "Holy shit!"

He grabbed his keys from the desk, turned off all

the lights, and locked up the house. The bathroom would wait until later. This was more important than some broken glass on the floor.

This could be the clue he and Lansing had been searching for.

18

A light rapping pulled Lansing from her emails. She had promised herself she would not get wrapped up in work more than once a week, but she had grown bored just sitting in her room, and had finished her book. She wasn't quite ready to venture far from her room after getting a good look at her bruises in the bathroom mirror.

"Come in," she said.

The door opened, and Tucker stepped inside. The room instantly felt a little brighter and a hell of a lot hotter. "Hey, how're you feeling?" he asked.

"Stir crazy," she said, and couldn't have stopped the silly grin that swept across her face if she had wanted to. "But I'm fully rested and feel good. Carmen brought me some lunch and a couple of pain relievers."

Tucker grimaced. "Did she see your neck?"

"Yes, but she didn't say anything. I was a little worried she might think you had done this to me because she asked where you were. I told her you went to find some answers about your family history, and she seemed to understand, but didn't ask any more questions."

"Probably doesn't want to know in case you tell her one of her ghosts tried to kill you and sue her."

Lansing snorted. "Yes, because a court will believe that a ghost attacked me in my sleep."

"Okay, okay, probably a stretch."

She glanced at a piece of paper he had clutched in his hand. "Find something interesting?"

"That's an understatement." He moved to the edge of the bed, sat across from her chair by the window, and handed her the picture.

Her pulse sped up. "Is that Eliza?"

"I'm pretty sure it is."

Adrenaline spiked through her body. "She's pregnant. Do you know who the child is?"

He handed her the paper. She peered at it. "A birth certificate?" She quickly scanned the document for the name of the child. "Calvin Augustus Cambridge." *Calvin*. The boy who played with the Cambridge children at the house?

Searching for the parent's names, a sudden chill filled her chest. "Maurice Cambridge and Eliza McGillicudy. So, they had a love child."

"It appears the childhood friend of Charles was actually his half-brother."

Heart racing, Lansing stood and walked toward the door. "I think we should go talk to Marjorie."

MARJORIE WAS in the kitchen prepping for dinner. She smiled when she saw Lansing and Tucker walk through the door. "Hello, you two. How are you feeling, Miss Lansing? Can I get you some hot tea?"

"Tea would be wonderful," Lansing replied.

Marjorie glanced at Tucker.

"No, thank you."

Marjorie pulled a china cup and saucer from the cabinet, placed a tea bag in it, and poured water from the steaming kettle on the stove. "Here you go," she said as she handed it to Lansing.

Lansing sat on one of the stools and let her bag steep. She peered at Marjorie, ready to gauge her reaction to the information they had uncovered. "Tucker found something interesting at Walter's house today."

"Is that right? What did you find?"

Tucker handed her the photo. "Looks like a picture of Eliza."

Marjorie's eyebrows drew together, creating deep creases at the bridge of her nose. "Yes, it does."

"Did you know she had a child?" Lansing asked. She removed the tea bag from her cup and placed it on the saucer.

Marjorie frowned and shook her head. "No, my mother never mentioned it, and I was so young when Eliza died that I barely remember her."

"So you have no idea who that child was?" Tucker asked.

"No, I'm sorry."

"Well, I do." Tucker handed her the birth certificate.

She read it slowly and then gasped. Her mouth dropped open, and she stared at Tucker with wide eyes. "I can't believe it."

"So, you really didn't know Calvin was Eliza's illegitimate son with Maurice?" Lansing asked. Marjorie did appear to be surprised. Could she just be that good a liar?

"I swear, I had no clue. Mother always said he was a friend of Charles's that came to play on the property."

"And you have no idea where he lived in town? Or who he lived with?" Tucker asked. A vein in his neck throbbed, and Lansing was sure he was holding his temper in check by a very tenuous string.

"No…I always wondered, but Mother would get so tense and upset when I would question her about Calvin or William that I stopped asking after a while."

Lansing stirred a spoonful of sugar into her cup, but remembered something Marjorie had told her in another conversation. "Didn't you say you used to see a woman and child on the property, and thought they lived in the cottage?"

"Yes, but Mother always denied it." Marjorie's hand went to the base of her necks and she fingered the pendant hanging from the chain. "You don't think—"

"That Calvin was the boy you saw? It's exactly what I think."

"I guess it is possible." She glanced back at the paper in her hand. "The age would be about right for the boy." She handed the picture and birth certificate back to Tucker. "But who was the woman I saw him with?"

"Good question," Tucker said. "There's only one person I know who can answer that."

WILLIAM KNELT before the headstone of his daughter, Delilah, and pulled at the grass that had grown at the base. He looked over his shoulder as Lansing and Tucker came into the clearing. A broad smile lit up his eyes when he saw Tucker. Slowly, he got to his feet and walked toward them.

"I didn't expect to see so soon. Hope you are feeling better, Miss." He nodded at Lansing.

She pulled the collar of her jacket up around her neck to conceal the marks. "Much better. Thank you."

"I was just tending to your great grandmother's grave." He gestured toward the headstone bearing Delilah's name. "It's nice to finally have a proper headstone in place—the old one did not have her name on it."

Tucker stepped toward the marker. Close by were the headstones for Maurice and Eliza. He pointed at Eliza's. "I know she had a son, and his name was Calvin. I suspect he's the same Calvin that played with Agatha, Charles, and Grandma Beaulah. Did he live here at the cottage?"

William dropped his head to his chest and nodded. "Yes."

"And you knew he was the half-brother of your grandchildren?"

"I thought it would be good for the children to meet and get to know each other. They really got along well—had so much fun running and playing on the property."

"Did *they* know they were related?"

"No, at the time they only knew that Calvin lived in the cottage. Vi hired a live-in nanny from Middleton who took care of him."

Tucker ran his hand over his face. "Didn't they ever question why Calvin and Marjorie didn't know each other?"

William shook his head. "They knew Vi was strict with Marjorie, and that she wasn't allowed to play with the boys or go outside of the gardens. I guess they just assumed that was the reason—if they thought of it at all. They were always too busy playing games and climbing trees to give much thought to anything else."

"Where is Calvin now?" Tucker asked.

William's shoulders tensed, and his body stiffened. He remained silent with his head down.

He doesn't want to tell us. Why? What could it hurt? Calvin had to be an old man—if he was even still alive.

Lansing sucked in her breath.

Of course! Why hadn't she seen it...Calvin is dead.

Lansing stared at the man for a moment longer. It all made sense. "Calvin is the boy buried under the tree, isn't he?"

Tucker's head whipped around, his eyebrows drawn together, but then his features softened as the pieces fell into place.

William exhaled and looked at Tucker. "Yes. No one knew him—no one would miss him—at least among the living."

"But he was so young—why would he kill himself?" Lansing asked.

William peered at Lansing, his stare drilling into her, making her feel as if she was an idiot. He shrugged and looked away. "Don't rightly know."

"But you must have thought about it. Considered the possibilities," Tucker said.

"Don't want to blame a child for the sins of the parents, but he was never supposed to be. Maybe he sensed it somehow. Was lonely not having a mother or father—can't speak for him. Just know I tried to care for him best I could." His face softened as he looked at Tucker. "He loved climbing on that tree—would go so high I thought he'd get stuck in the clouds. I guess I reckoned he'd like to stay close to it."

Lansing glanced at Tucker. He shook his head, his eyes searching for what to do next. They needed a chance to absorb all the information. She pointed toward the inn, and he nodded, and stepped closer to her. Grasping her hand, he tightened his grip as they turned to walk away.

Lansing halted and stared back at William.

"Calvin is the little boy I've been seeing, isn't he?"

William nodded. "Suppose he is."

19

Tucker and Lansing ate dinner in silence. He pondered all they had uncovered. Following Lansing to her room, he closed the door behind him, plopped down on the bed next to her, and leaned back against the headboard.

"So, Calvin is Eliza's son and is buried under the tree. That solves one mystery," Tucker said, releasing a long, heavy sigh.

"Two," Lansing corrected him.

He glanced at her and raised an eyebrow.

"The little boy at Walter's house is Calvin."

"And I'd bet assholes to nuts he's Agatha and Charles' ghost, also."

Lansing rolled onto her side, propped up her head with her hand, and faced him. "But why is Calvin haunting Delilah's children?"

Tucker's mind raced through all the options. "Marjorie said the Cambridge children stopped coming to visit after a while. Maybe Calvin was upset because he was alone again."

"Then took his life." Lansing stared straight ahead

and was quiet for a moment. "And haunted them because they left him?"

Tucker shook his head. Something about that didn't feel right. "Charles said something that has bothered me. He was happy Beaulah had been spared. So Calvin and Agatha must have been the only two Calvin preyed upon."

"So Calvin haunted Agatha into insanity and she jumped to her death—but then why was he haunting her?"

"And Charles?"

"Plus, it still doesn't answer why Cora died?"

Rubbing the back of his neck, Tucker drew in a long, deep breath and released it before speaking. "Calvin wouldn't have any reason to haunt her—would he?"

"I can't imagine why. He'd died way before she was born."

"And she was Beaulah's daughter, and Beaulah wasn't one of Calvin's haunting victims."

"So, could it just be a coincidence that Cora died in the same place as Agatha, on the anniversary of her death, and in the exact manner?"

"Her death was ruled a suicide and there was discussion of mental instability."

Lansing tilted her head slightly to one side. "Yeah, the same 'mental instability' Agatha suffered from, so it is possible she took her own life." She used air quotes to make her point.

"There was some question about whether or not Cora had been murdered." Every muscle in Tucker's body strained. He rolled his shoulders to relieve some of the tension.

"Who would have murdered her?" Lansing asked.

"The same person who tried to murder you."

Lansing paled and Tucker regretted bringing up memories of Eliza strangling her. That last thing he wanted was to see fear and apprehension in Lansing's gorgeous green eyes. He grabbed her hand, and tugged her arm until she snuggled into his side and rested her head on his chest. He wanted to protect her from everything, including painful memories. But, more than that, he needed her close—to feel her next him. Somehow, she had gotten under his skin, and the idea of there being any distance between them made his stomach twist in a knot.

"Why would Eliza want to kill Cora?" Her voice lowered almost to a whisper.

"Opportunity—she was there—and Eliza was mourning the death of her child?"

"I guess...but this just gets more curious with every revelation."

That was an understatement. Tucker hadn't imagined getting embroiled in a family mystery when he'd agreed to come to Chistine. But here he was, and the way information was trickling in and only creating more questions made him wonder if they would ever uncover the truth.

Lansing yawned, but quickly covered her mouth with her hand. "Excuse me," she said, her smile wide, brightening her gorgeous eyes. "Sorry, that was rude."

Tucker needed to leave so she could get some sleep after the hellish night she'd had. If he stayed, he wasn't sure he could actually get through a second night of gentlemanly behavior sharing a bed with her. Though, the thought of not sleeping with her—her body snuggled up against his, head resting on his chest, the melodic sound of her breathing as she slept—nearly crushed him. He gave her the best smile he could muster. "I should go."

Her face turned ashen and her lips trembled. "Can you stay? I know you probably didn't get very much sleep last night, but…it's just…God, this is so embarrassing—"

"You're nervous you may get another visit from Eliza." Tucker's heart expanded, but his chest tightened. He loved that she wanted him to stay, but hated that she was afraid.

She nodded. "How pathetic is that? I'm a grown woman who's afraid of the dark."

He lifted her chin with his finger and forced her to look at him. "After what you endured, I'd say you're handling all of this better than expected. I don't know how all this after death stuff happens, but those marks on your neck are proof that you are lucky to have escaped Eliza with your life. It's one thing to be attacked and nearly choked to death, but then to have to come to grips with the realization that it was at the hands of a ghost while you were dreaming—I think we're lucky you aren't curled in the fetal position muttering incoherently."

She smiled and huffed out a chuckle. He prided himself in being able to make her laugh. *God, she was an amazing woman.*

"But pathetic? That's not how I would describe you at all."

All he could concentrate on was the brilliant green of her eyes bathing him in sensuous heat. She reached up and rested her hand against his cheek. It was a simple caress, but he felt her in every part of his body, and the need to touch her was unquenchable. He leaned forward, his lips pressing against hers. She ran her fingers through his hair, and fire burned through him. He deepened the kiss, licking the seam of her lips, and pushing his tongue inside her mouth. Rolling her onto her back, he rested his leg in between hers. His hand traced her smooth skin, outlining the curve of her hip, memorizing the dip at her waist. Cupping her breast, he squeezed until she moaned.

He wanted to take his time, make this moment last forever, discover every inch of silky skin. But he was hungry and she was delectable.

He gazed into her eyes, dark and dilated. Her lips were wet and swollen from kissing. Her chest heaved from panting. She held his gaze, speaking to him with her eyes, letting him know she was giving into him.

"You know this is more than just sex, right? This means more to me—you mean more to me—" He needed her to understand he was emotionally invested in her.

"Yes." Her voice was breathy. "I know."

Clothes were stripped and tossed onto the floor. Tucker positioned himself between her legs, his erection pressing into her thigh. He bent his head and took her nipple into his mouth, lathing the tip with his tongue. She moaned and arched her back, forcing more of her breast into his mouth. A light sheen covered her skin, and her scent was like an electric current zapping his nerves.

His hand moved between her legs, finding her slick silkiness, and forcing a deep groan from his chest. She tore open the condom wrapper and handed it to him. Quickly sheathing himself, he pressed her knees up and slid into her, pushing as deep as he could go.

"Oh my god," she murmured, her hands clutching his arms. She arched her back, and dug her heels into his buttocks, forcing him deeper inside her. He moved in and out of her, slowly at first, but as the heat built between them, the pace increased. With every thrust inside, she gasped, and he knew he had found the spot that sent spikes of pleasure through her. Every pant made him want more of her—all of her. Stars danced in front of his eyes, and pressure built in his cock.

She gasped, and clamped her muscles around him. Her body pulsed, her mouth opened, and a long, satisfied moan filled his ears. It was the sweetest music he'd ever heard.

Tucker exploded inside her, his body tingling. He collapsed on top of her, and rolled to his side, wrapping his arms around her. He kissed her temple and she tucked her head under his chin. Within a few minutes, he heard her soft, steady breathing. She had drifted off to sleep. *Good.* She needed a decent night's sleep, and he was going to make sure nothing harmed her during the night. Or ever again.

He wanted more of her, more of everything. The sex, the intimacy. Tucker was in over his head, and, oddly, it was exactly where he wanted to be.

THE ROOM WAS BATHED in moonlight. Tucker lay in Lansing's bed, staring up at the ceiling, listening to her soft breathing as she slept. He was…content. This had to be the first time in his life he hadn't gotten out of bed, dressed, and left whatever woman he had just screwed without anything more than a thanks and a good-bye. No promises to call, no desires to see them in the future, not even a 'see you around'. But being here with Lansing, staying after the most incredibly intimate sex of his life, seemed normal. The thought of getting up and going back to his room—the need to distance himself from her after sharing such an intense connection—didn't even cross his mind. The idea seemed almost sacrilegious somehow, like a sin against the exclusiveness of what they had together.

He closed his eyes. Sleep seemed just out of his reach. Too many thoughts bounced around in his head, too many tasks to be prioritized. Too many dreams throwing him off. A tap against the glass caught his attention. He stilled, listening through the silence. There it was again. Something hit the window. When he heard it a third time, he slipped out of bed, and crossed the room to the window.

Movement in the garden caught his eye. Stepping from the shadows onto the path was the little boy he'd seen at his Uncle Walter's house. The boy they presumed was Calvin's ghost. He waved at Tucker, gesturing for him to come to the garden. Tucker froze for a moment, contemplating.

He glanced at Lansing, sleeping soundly, and caught a glimpse of the bruises on her neck. The little boy hadn't shown any violent tendencies towards them, but did that mean he wouldn't? So far, he hadn't haunted them mercilessly. His mother, on the other hand, was a wannabe murderer. The boy was trying to help them uncover clues to his death. Didn't Tucker owe it to Calvin to find out what happened? After all, they were related.

Tucker pulled on his jeans and t-shirt, and slipped his feet into his shoes. He hesitated at the door, and peered at Lansing. What if Eliza came after Lansing again and he wasn't there to wake her?

He had to believe Eliza would see Tucker was helping her son and leave Lansing alone. The boy was trying to show him something. He quietly descended the stairs, and slipped out the back door to the gardens.

20

Lansing rolled over and reached her arm across the bed for Tucker and was met with a cold sheet instead of a warm chest. She opened her eyes and confirmed he was not in the bed. Lifting her head, she glanced around the room but he wasn't there, either. Had he left her in the middle of the night to go back to his room? Did he regret making love to her?

She recalled his scent, spicy and male, that made her dizzy. The way the muscles in his arms, shoulders and jaw tensed when her core clenched around him. But it was the look on his face—the dreamy, intense glaze of his eyes—that confirmed what was transpiring between them was much more than sex. A tether, deep and taut, tied them together. She hadn't imagined it, he felt it, too. It was there, after, the way he held her, placed kisses on her forehead as his fingers ran through her hair. How he drew her arm across his chest and held her tightly to him, as if she may escape if he let her go.

Not that she would have. She would've stayed in that position forever, if he had asked. She had never been one to believe in what romance novels peddled—instant affection and deep connections within the first two chapters. She allowed herself to get lost in those stories, but was very much grounded in the reality that there was no such thing as love at first sight.

She flung her arm over her eyes, and chuckled in exasperation. *Love?* She didn't love Tucker. It was way too soon for that. She barely knew anything about him. But there was no denying the connection between them. She had felt so comfortable with him since they first met. Everything that happened between them was a surprise, but also felt as if it was meant to be. It never felt odd—there was never a period of adjustment—it just felt…right.

So, if everything is so right, where is he?

Swinging her legs over the side of the bed, she walked to the armoire and grabbed her robe off the hook. She glanced out the window, but even with an unobstructed moon lighting the gardens, it was dark. The residents of Chistine slept. The living ones, anyway.

But what about the dead?

She knew from the stories about the inn that William, stuck as he was in limbo between the living and dead, did not sleep. So, where were the ghostly occupants of Silent Cove?

Lansing glanced at the door. Should she lock it? For what, to keep Tucker out? She doubted any ethereal presence would be stopped by a locked door.

Pulling her robe tight around her, she attempted to stave off the sudden chill at the thought of being revisited by Eliza. There was no way she would get back to sleep now, not without Tucker here. Even if she was able to fall asleep, Lansing wasn't about to give

Eliza the opportunity to enter her dreams and attack her again.

Turning on the lamp by the window, she pulled Agatha's journals from the desk and curled up in the chair.

"Let's see when you started slipping into insanity, Agatha."

Several envelopes fell from the back cover of the book and landed on Lansing's lap. She flipped through them. All were addressed to Charles at an APO address. Each letter had "return to sender" scrawled across them in unsteady handwriting, and the seal on the back was still intact.

So, Charles never read the letters his sister sent him while he was in the Army? And worse, refused to even accept them?

Lansing slipped her finger under the envelope flap and slid out the yellowing paper.

"Why would you do that, Charles? What were you afraid to read?"

21

Calvin seemed to glow in the moonlight as Tucker's eyes adjusted to the darkness in the garden. The moon made it easier to follow the path, but it was still damn dark. And the shadows the moonlight created could have come straight from a Stephen King novel. Of course, Tucker's skittishness might be due to the fact he was meeting a known ghost in the middle of the night. Given what Eliza had done to Lansing, there was reason to wonder if the shadows were actually real or hands reaching out to snag him and drag him into the pits of hell.

When Tucker was about ten feet from the boy, the boy turned and walked to the edge of the garden. He glanced over his shoulder at Tucker, and gestured for him to follow.

"Where are you taking me?" Tucker asked, but the boy just turned and walked into the trees. "Fuck." Tucker followed the spirit.

The branches formed a canopy over the trail, and blocked out the moon. Luckily, Tucker had the foresight to grab the flashlight that hung from a hook beside the back door of the inn. He pulled it out of his pocket, pushed the button, and was surprised at how much light the small torch provided. He aimed the beam down along the trail. If he lifted it, he couldn't see Calvin very well.

They rounded the bend and passed by the tree where Calvin had hung himself. Tucker thought maybe the boy had something to show him at his grave, but they continued down the path toward the cottage. There must be something about the graves at the cottage that Calvin needed to show him, but what? Maybe it had something to do with William? He lived out there, if he could be considered among the living. Or something about Eliza.

At the fork where the two paths dissected, Calvin veered away from the cottage. He was leading Tucker to the cliff. Tucker's heart rate accelerated. Nothing good had ever come from a Cambridge family member going to that particular spot. The two members of the family he knew of had gone over the edge and met untimely deaths. The marks on Lansing's neck reminded Tucker that ghosts were not the wisps of nothingness Hollywood depicted. They were physically able to inflict pain.

Lansing said she had tried to stop Eliza but was unable to grip the woman's wrists. What would Tucker do if Calvin attacked him?

Nothing...except die.

But why would the boy want to hurt Tucker? It wasn't as if Tucker had been around when Calvin had been killed. Was it simply because he was a descendent of Charles? Surely not. Charles had remarked that Beaulah had been spared. And nothing indicated that

Walter had died of anything other than natural causes. But Cora...if the rumors were true, she was pushed to her death. Had Calvin killed both Agatha and Cora in the same manner?

Was Tucker next on his list?

22

Dear Charles,

I HOPE the Army is treating you well. I think about you every day and pray you return home safely. I, myself, am in constant agony since you left. Beaulah has tried to improve my state, but she does not understand what I suffer. She was not present that awful night. She did not see…

Please write me back at your earliest convenience.
Love, your devoted sister,
Agatha

LANSING FOLDED THE LETTER, replaced it in the envelope, and opened the next one.

DEAR CHARLES,

WHY DID you leave me here? Alone? To face him on my

own? I can't get what we did out of my mind. He comes to me in my dreams. He whispers to me, and tells me the most horrible things. He says he will never rest until we pay for what we have done. I no longer sleep. I know you said he was a threat to our family, that he would take everything and leave us with nothing if anyone found out about him. But I can do nothing but endlessly ponder whether we did the right thing.

Love,
   Agatha

Dear Charles,

I see him everywhere. *He talks to me while I sleep. He follows me while I am awake. He says he will kill me. Kill both of us. He wants to see the fear in our eyes as we die.*
   I can't take this anymore.
   I can't...

Lansing inhaled deeply, set the letters on the table, and stood in front of the window. There was a lot of information in the letters. The picture was clearing, but still murky. Did Charles and Agatha drive Calvin to commit suicide somehow? Did they see him as a threat? According to William, Agatha, Beaulah, and Charles had no idea Calvin was their half brother. So why would they see him as a threat?

And what had they said or done to him to make him want to hang himself from his favorite climbing tree?

There were no answers...yet. But Lansing was determined to figure this out. If only Tucker would return so she could run everything by him. Maybe he would have some insight she was unable to see.

A light glowed from the distance in the area of the cliff where Agatha and Cora had lost their lives. Perhaps some sort of beacon for ships. Lansing hadn't noticed anything previously, but then, she hadn't really paid much attention, either.

Sighing, she returned to her seat, and grabbed the last letter in the stack. The postmark was a few years after the other letters, and the address was his home in Middleton.

Dear Charles,

Since you refuse to see me or speak to me on the phone, I can only hope this letter reaches you and that you will read it. I am not holding out much hope since you have returned all my letters to date. There is no hope for me. I can no longer avoid my fate. I am at peace with what will become of me.

I cannot escape him. He is everywhere and in everything I do and see. I must accept what he has prophesized.

He did not deserve what we did to him.

He was our brother.

Goodbye,
  Agatha

They knew...they knew Calvin was their half brother.

At least Agatha and Charles did. And they forced him to commit suicide to avoid being discovered.

But *why*?

Lansing glanced toward the window. Where was Tucker? Should she go look for him?

Maybe he saw something...or someone. Eliza? Or Calvin?

"Oh my God!" Lansing sat up, her hand covered her mouth as her brain kicked in. *The light out at the cliff.*

Grabbing a pair of lounging pants and a sweater, she slid her feet into her running shoes and headed out the door. She knew where Tucker was.

And she knew what would happen if she didn't reach him in time.

LANSING RAN through the forest toward the cliff. She prayed she would make it in time. Tears filled her eyes, blurring her vision. She swiped them away. No time for tears. She couldn't afford to slow down. Tucker needed her.

She broke through the trees into the clearing. Tucker was at the edge of the cliff. He teetered dangerously close to the rim.

"Tucker!"

He didn't flinch.

A screeching howl filled the night air. Razor sharp pain sliced down her back. Twisting, Lansing saw Eliza a few feet away. Her eyes were aflame, her teeth bared, and her nails primed and in position to strike again.

"Calvin, please, stop this!" Lansing cried.

The boy turned his vacant gaze toward her, but said nothing.

"Tucker is innocent," she implored. "Why are you doing this to him?"

A heavy weight dropped onto her shoulders. Eliza's arm slipped around Lansing's neck. She tried to pry it away, but it was useless.

"I heard him...at the house."

Lansing stared at the boy. It was the first time he'd spoken.

"What did you hear?" Lansing managed to choke out the words.

"He said he was going to keep the house."

"I don't understand. Why do you want to hurt him for that?"

"They killed me because of the house. They didn't want me to live there with them. They were ashamed of me, and didn't want me as their brother. They thought I would take what was theirs. But I wouldn't have...I just wanted a family." He looked down at his feet and kicked at the dirt. "I was so lonely."

Eliza was still clinging to her, but had loosened her hold around Lansing's neck.

"But they didn't kill you," Lansing said. "You killed yourself."

"No," Calvin said, his eyes narrowed and his face scrunched up and twisted. "They tricked me."

Lansing glanced at Tucker, still tottering on the edge of the cliff, staring at the dark water below. Completely oblivious to the conversation. Was he in a trance? Had he been sleepwalking?

"Please, he had no idea that wanting to keep the house would upset you. If he had, he wouldn't have considered it. In fact, I bet if he knew all that had happened to you, he wouldn't want anything more to do with the house. Please—please don't hurt him."

The weight was suddenly lifted from Lansing. Eliza

let out a blood-curdling scream. Lansing whirled around. Eliza was flat on her back on the ground. Hovering over her was William, his foot in the center of her chest, holding her down.

Lansing took advantage of the attention being off her, and darted toward Tucker. If she could grasp his arm, she could pull him away from the edge. Back to safety.

But Calvin stepped in front of her, and put out his hand. She halted as if she had hit a brick wall.

"Calvin," William said. "Let Tucker be."

"Give him the opportunity to make this right," Lansing added.

Calvin glanced at William then at Lansing and shook his head. "He can't make it right. There is only one thing that can make this right. Only one person."

"Who?" Lansing asked.

"Me."

A male voice, low and deep, wafted from the darkness. A feeble old man stepped out of the trees.

"You don't need to hurt the young man," Charles said. "Let him go."

23

"Tucker!"

Tucker woke from his dream. Glancing around, he expected to find himself in bed beside Lansing. Instead, he was beside the cliff.

What the fuck?

He stumbled backwards. What the hell was he doing out here? And why was he so close to the edge of the cliff?

Lansing threw her arms around his neck and he caught her body as she slammed against his chest.

"Thank god you're okay," she whimpered into his neck.

"I don't understand," he murmured. "How did I get here?"

"Calvin brought you."

Images flooded his vision. Everything was foggy, like a dream he couldn't quite grasp and hold onto, dissipating like smoke. He'd been following Calvin into the woods. "Why?"

"Because of me. Because of what I did to him."

Charles? His mind raced to tie together all the loose ends. Sweat dripped down his back.

No one said anything. Tucker was the only one in the dark about what the hell was going on. "Someone want to fill me in on the secret?"

"He was jealous," Eliza sneered.

"No," Charles said, and glared at the woman. He looked at Calvin. Sadness seeped from his eyes. "I was scared. I heard my grandmother talking to Vi, telling her that no one could know that Calvin was Maurice's son."

"But why?" Tucker asked.

"Because he would have a claim to part of Maurice's estate," Lansing answered.

Charles nodded. "I didn't understand what that meant, but I understood her weeping as she talked to a photo of Grandpa. She said Calvin would take everything from them. We would be homeless and poor. I didn't understand how, but I trusted Grandmother Zora. She was all we had left, and I was the man of the family. I had to protect us no matter what."

"What did you do?" Tucker asked.

"I snuck out one night, and rode my bike over here. I tapped on Calvin's window and told him to get dressed and come outside. I had a surprise for him. He believed me—*why wouldn't he?*—we were best friends." Tears leaked out the corners of his eyes and trailed down his face. "I took him to his favorite tree, and we sat on the sturdiest branch, like we had so many times before."

"I asked what the surprise was, and he just smiled at me. Then I saw the rope being flung over the branch from below." Calvin's young voice seemed out of place in such a serious conversation. No child should have to talk about death—especially not his own.

"Agatha," Lansing said. "She was there. She helped you."

Charles nodded. "Yes, she was always a little mouse--would follow me everywhere—even though she was the oldest. She was a second mother to Beaulah and I. I noticed her when I was at the cottage. I told her we were going to play a harmless prank on Calvin. We did stuff like that all the time." His eyes softened and a pained smile tipped up the corners of his mouth as he gazed at his half-brother. "You wouldn't have thought anything of it."

"How did you get the noose around his neck?" Lansing asked.

"I convinced him we were going to play a prank on Grandpa. Calvin would have the noose around his neck and it would look like he had hung himself from the tree. I convinced him I would make sure the noose was not tight, and that Agatha and I would hold his legs so he didn't have any weight on his neck."

"It was gonna be the best prank ever," Calvin said, his voice filled with childlike exuberance.

"I helped him put the noose around his neck. I kept it loose, at first, but then I pulled it as tight as I could—" Charles buried his face in his hands—"And pushed him off the branch."

Sobs wracked his body, and he fell to his knees.

Holy shit. Tucker dragged his hand down his face. Ice sluiced painfully through his veins. His head pounded, and his heart seized in his chest. So much unnecessary heartache and death. "But why did Agatha have to pay? She didn't have any idea Charles was planning to kill you. She thought it was all in good fun, just like you."

"She didn't stop him," Eliza screamed, pointing a finger at Charles. "She could've helped my poor baby, but she just stood there. She could've tried to get him down from the tree, but she just watched as my darling son struggled to get free until he finally couldn't breathe any longer."

"Did you push Agatha off the cliff?" Tucker asked Calvin.

The little boy shook his head. "No, not her. She came to the tree. She was crying and begging me to tell her what she could do to make it up to me." Calvin looked at Charles then Tucker. "I told her to jump off the cliff, and she did."

Tucker's knees trembled under the weight of what Calvin had said. Agatha must have been ruthlessly tormented if the only way out was jumping into the rocky cove.

"You said, 'not her'. What do you mean by that?" Lansing asked.

"The other girl, Cora, she came here to put flowers by the cliff. She was sad. She was saying things—talking to Agatha as if she was here."

"What was she saying?"

"That she was sorry Agatha died. That she didn't understand why she would kill herself—that nothing was so bad that she could've done that." Calvin's dark eyes flamed. "But she was wrong! She felt bad for Agatha when she should've felt bad for me. She brought flowers for Agatha, but no one ever gave me flowers. No one ever came to my grave to tell me they were sorry for my death."

"What did you do?" Tucker asked, but he wasn't sure how much more he could take. No wonder his father hadn't wanted to be around his family.

"She had white roses she was dropping over the

side into the water. I pushed her, but she grabbed onto a tree branch. So, I poked her in the eyes. She screamed and let go."

Bile rose in Tucker's throat. So much suffering over something so meaningless. Something that wouldn't have mattered, even if the secret of Calvin's parentage had been revealed. "She died for no reason. Do you understand what you did? My father refused to have anything more to do with his family after that. He barely spoke to his only brother. And Walter died alone."

"I died. All I wanted was a family. But my family didn't want me. Why should they be happy?"

Lansing inhaled beside him, her breath ragged, as if she was close to breaking down. "And you were going to kill Tucker because he wanted to maintain that familial link by keeping the house?"

"I saw him—when he would talk about keeping the house—he was happy. No one was going to be happy in that house."

"Ever?"

"Not until I get retribution for what was done to me."

Tucker knew what that meant. There was one person—the one person who had started this downward spiral of death—who had not yet paid.

Charles.

Standing on the edge of the cliff, Charles gazed at Calvin. "I know I don't have the right to ask for your forgiveness, and you have no reason to believe me when I say that I am so very sorry for what I did. I was young, and stupid, and did something I wish I could've taken back. You will never know how much I regretted my actions. Not just because I killed you, but I also missed you."

Tucker watched the man closely. Charles was too close to the edge. One step to his left and he would slip over the side. "We need to get him away from there," Tucker whispered to Lansing.

She glanced at Charles, nodded, and moved a little closer to the man.

Charles's head jerked toward her. "Don't come any closer."

Tucker and Lansing froze.

"I'm so sorry," Charles said to Calvin, his eyes glistening in the moonlight. "I'm ready to do what I should have done many years ago." He looked at Tucker. "Please tell Penelope that I love her. She deserved better than me. She should've had a family, children and grandchildren. I don't know if she will ever forgive me, but I did try to give her a happy life—such as it was. But her sacrifices were many, and she paid for my sins. I wasn't strong enough to let her live the life she should've had, and for that I am eternally sorry."

Tucker rushed forward. He reached for Charles's arm. The old man pivoted, stepped off the edge, and disappeared over the side.

"No!" Tucker darted to the edge. Charles had plunged into the swirling surf and ragged rocks below.

Tucker's foot slipped on the loose dirt. He fell to one knee, and his foot dangled over the side. Twisting his upper body, he placed both hands on the ground to lift his body. His other foot went out from under him.

He slipped over the cliff.

Everything was moving too fast. He was able to see every movement with great clarity. He was sliding. Next he would tumble then become airborne, and plummet into the cove. Which would he hit first—the water or the rocks? Would he lose consciousness during the fall or would it be after he hit the cold, hard water? Would death come quickly and painlessly? Or would he feel every torturous moment leading up to the inevitable?

He grasped the exposed root of a century old tree. His hands were sweaty. His grip slowly slipped along the root. Peering over his shoulder at the angry swell below him, regret seized his chest. He would never see his family again. He would never know if he and Lansing could have built a relationship, a family--a life together.

"No!"

Lansing's body flew through the air toward him. She landed a foot away, her arms outstretched.

Thank god those beautiful green eyes will be the last thing I see before I die.

"Take my hand." Her words had no meaning to him, at first. It was as if they had to seep into his body, flow through his veins until they finally reached his brain and had meaning. She was offering him a lifeline. A way to have the things he wanted. If he could just get to her...

Her hand remained just out of his grasp. He scrambled to get up the side of the cliff, but the dirt was not stable enough for him to get traction. His body slid over the rocks. The path to his death was going to be a slow and painful tumble down the side of the cliff before he struck the rocks that jutted from the water. After that, it wouldn't matter if he went into the water or not. The impact against the rocks was certain to kill him.

Maybe I should just let go, and try to fling myself as far out as I can? Avoid hitting the rocks and succumb to the water... It sounded like a much better option than tumbling over stones and branches until his body slammed against the rocks.

He planted his feet against the side, and bent his knees so he could launch away from the cliffside.

"Tucker Kingsley, don't you even consider leaving me."

Lansing. She twisted her fingers around his. He knew it wouldn't be enough to hold him. God, he hated disappointing her. He hated that she was going to have to watch him fall to his death.

"None of this is your fault," he said. The last thing he wanted was for her to go through life feeling guilty about his untimely death. He just failed to see any way out of the inevitable. "Live a happy life for both of us."

"Bullshit." Fire flamed in her eyes. "You fight, dammit! You get your ass up here and take me on a proper date. You owe me, Tucker Kingsley."

There was fierceness in her voice. Anger fueled confidence, as if she was willing a different outcome than the one he had predicted. Daring him to defy her demands. Everything about her in that moment—everything she had done for him, how she had made him feel, the desire to have more in his future than his career and one night stands—gave him strength to dig in. To climb up the cliff. To get to her and make sure she knew he would always be there for her. And that he would never choose death over one minute with her.

He released one hand from the tree root, and thrust it at her. She held on with both hands and tried to pull him up. But she was still on her stomach along the ground. She had no leverage. He kicked the toe of his shoe into the side of the cliff, and tried to gain a foothold. He had to get back to her. She wanted him—he could see it in her eyes—clear down into her soul.

Her hands were sweaty. He slipped through them. She grabbed him again, squeezing his hand. But there was no way she was going to be able to pull one-hundred and seventy five pounds up the hill without some assistance.

And he wasn't sure how much he was going to be able to help. Life seemed like a cruel joke, dangling happiness in front of him, making him crave something he had never even considered was missing from his life, only to take it all away before he had a chance to savor the sweet nectar of a life.

"Lansing," he said, suddenly needing to tell her how he felt before it was too late. "I think I love you. I've never been in love before, so I'm not sure what I'm feeling, but if I had to name it—it would be love. I know we've only just met, and that we still have so much to learn about each other—but if I could only have one wish come true—it would be to spend the rest of my life with you."

A warm breeze enveloped him. Hands grasped his upper arms, and pulled him up the cliff side. He peered into the face of a woman—young and pretty. She smiled, and he recognized her immediately. "Cora?"

She nodded and looked past him. On the other side of him was another woman, this one a little older, but with the same eyes and smile. "Aunt Agatha."

They hauled him up and over the side to safety. Tucker grabbed Lansing by the shoulders, yanked her body against his, and buried his face in her neck. He wanted to stay right there, inhaling the sweet smell of vanilla mixed with sea salt and sweat that moistened her skin. Her arms wrapped around his neck, and she ducked her head down until their noses touched. Her lips pressed against his for what seemed like minutes.

When she finally released him, he dragged in a deep breath, his fingers running through her hair.

"I thought I was going to lose you," she said.

Tucker kissed her, hard, branding her as his for as long as she would have him. Feet shuffled around them, and he remembered they were not alone.

Standing before him were the two women who had saved him. "Thank you," he said. "I don't know how I will ever repay you for saving my life."

They smiled, their bodies dissipating like the early morning mist.

Slipping his arm around Lansing's waist, he pulled her close into his side. Her warmth saturated him like a warm blanket on a cold night. Every part of his body tingled from her proximity.

Glancing around, Tucker noticed that only William remained. "Where did everyone go?"

"They have gone to their final resting place," William said.

"All of them?" Lansing asked.

William nodded.

"Even Agatha and Cora?" Tucker asked.

"Yes," William said.

"But not you?" Lansing asked the old man.

The corners of his eyes dipped down. "I will not be free until my darling Delilah can find peace and accept her death. Until then, my existence is tied to hers."

Lansing reached her hand toward him, but stopped before she actually touched him. "I'm so very sorry, William."

"Thank you, my dear." He glanced at Tucker and smiled. "It is not all bad. I have been able to meet my great, great grandson. I hope to see more of you in the future."

Tucker didn't even have to think about his answer.

"I'll visit every chance I get. And I might even be able to convince my dad to come along—although explaining to him how this is all possible might land me in a psych ward."

William laughed. "Well, you get him here, and I will help you talk to him. It's hard to deny someone's existence when they are standing in front of you." He winked, turned, and disappeared through the trees.

Tucker turned to Lansing, his hands on her hips. "Crazy night."

"Crazy week," she corrected. "But I will tell you this, if I wake up in the morning and find out it was all a dream, I'm going to be pissed."

"Well, we better make the most of the rest of the night, then, don't you think?" Tucker asked, and pressed his lips against hers.

"Yes," she murmured and sighed. "Yes, I do."

Lacing his fingers with hers, he turned and led her down the path toward the inn. The sun was just beginning to peek over the horizon, painting the sky in a brilliant orange. By the time they got back to the house, the lights were on in the downstairs, and they could see Carmen and Marjorie flitting around the kitchen like synchronized dancers preparing breakfast.

"Looks like we made it through the night," Lansing said.

"Yes, it does," Tucker agreed. "You know what this means, don't you? It means that everything was real."

"Not that anyone in their right minds would believe it."

EPILOGUE

One month later...

LANSING FOLLOWED the funeral procession down the path from the giant oak tree toward the cottage. Tucker and Angelo, Carmen's husband, balanced a small maple box on their shoulders. Inside lay Calvin's remains. Marjorie walked between Carmen and Lansing, her arms linked through theirs. Carmen had offered to drive the woman to the cottage in the golf cart, but Marjorie insisted on walking.

They stepped out from under the forest canopy into the bright sunshine. William stood next to a deep hole in the ground. Calvin's coffin was lowered into the grave next to where his mother, Eliza, now rested in peace.

Tucker glanced at Lansing. "Could you say a few words before we continue?"

Lansing nodded and squeezed his hand. "This is long overdue. Calvin, your time on this earth was short, and while you faced a tragic end, the life you did have was happy. It is always sad when a child dies, and your presence here after your death was marred by sadness, unrest, and violence. We hope you have finally the peace you so desperately deserve in your new resting place."

She tossed the rose she held into his grave and stepped aside so Tucker could do the same. One-by-one, the mourners paid their respects to the little boy. William plunged his shovel into the pile of dirt and filled in the grave.

Tucker took Lansing's hand and they strolled back toward the inn. It had been a simple ceremony, but necessary. He was where he needed to be—in the family cemetery close to his mother. Eliza may not have been there for the boy while he was alive, but she was his fiercest ally in death. It seemed only fitting that Calvin should be buried next to her.

"Do you think they have all 'gone into the light' or crossed over…or whatever spirits are supposed to do to move on?" Tucker asked.

Lansing shrugged. "Carmen and William haven't seen any of the ghosts in a while—except for Delilah. She doesn't appear to be going anywhere for a while."

Tucker touched the amulet pinned to his lapel. "Yeah, I was a little worried she would make an appearance today and cause an uproar."

"I think that's why Carmen and Marjorie were constantly asking everyone if they were wearing their ghost repellent jewelry."

They walked down the path in silence, swinging their hands back-and-forth between them like young lovers. The past month had been as exciting as discovering the truth about Calvin and his death—albeit, a different kind of excitement. Tucker decided to keep the family home in Chistine, and set about making some renovations and repairs. Lansing split her time between writing and helping Tucker. At the end of the second week, Tucker returned to Boston and his job. Lansing stayed in Chistine and worked on her book while keeping an eye on the construction being done at the house.

Every weekend Tucker would return, and the two would spend as much time together as possible. And Lansing couldn't have been happier. At one time she had thought Tucker was nothing more than a rich businessman with a fear of commitment. He admitted to her recently that he was exactly how she had perceived him. But all that changed once he met her.

Heat bloomed in her chest whenever she thought about him telling her that she had changed his outlook on commitment and relationships. He wanted her, and she wanted to make sure he never felt any differently.

The giant oak tree came into view, and they stopped in front of it. "Such a grand tree—so beautiful and majestic. It's sad to think about it being used as a deadly weapon against a child," Lansing said.

"Hopefully, if Carmen and Angelo ever have kids, they will be able to negate some of the tragedy and enjoy it the way Calvin seemed to while he was growing up."

Lansing hoped so, too. Little-by-little, with some tender loving care, Carmen and Angelo were transforming Silent Cove into a beautiful and inviting getaway.

Tucker clasped her hand in both of his. "So, something has been nagging at me for a while, and I think it's time to address it." He released a drawn-out sigh. "When I was hanging over the side of the cliff, and I thought all hope was lost—I said something to you. At the time, I thought it was true, but now that I've had time to reflect, I need to set things straight."

"O-kay." Lansing's heart plummeted into her stomach with a thud. He was about to drop a bombshell of disappointment that she was not prepared for, and had been hoping to avoid. But she knew what was coming...

"I told you that I thought I was falling in love with you—that wasn't exactly accurate."

The air around them stilled, and Lansing found it hard to breathe. She wanted to run away before he had a chance to tell her what she had been dreading—that he wasn't falling in love with her. He'd jumped the gun, thought he was going to die, and made a declaration of love while he could.

"What I have been wanting to say since that day was that I'm not falling in love with—I'm already there."

Her head snapped up and she stared at him. Had she heard him right?

"I know this is crazy. I know it's too soon. But I also know what I feel. True, deep, bubbling up from the bottom of my soul love. The kind of love that makes a man say things he hopes are romantic but are more often than not just plain goofy."

Lansing laughed. Words were flying out of Tucker's mouth fast enough to break the sound barrier. She hadn't ever seen him this flustered before.

He rested his hand on her hips. "I know this is going to be challenging—you live in Rhode Island and I live in Boston—but there has to be some way to work it out so we can see each other."

"I'm on sabbatical through the summer, so I can be flexible."

"Good to know," he said, waggling his eyebrows.

She smacked him on the arm. "Not that kind of flexible, perv."

He laughed. "And after that, we can spend weekends together—at your place, mine, or even here in Chistine."

Lansing thought about his proposal for a minute. It seemed doomed for failure. Only seeing each other on the weekends. Living separate lives during the week—it was a recipe for a failed relationship. "I don't think I can do that."

Tucker's face dropped. "What? Have a long distance relationship with me?"

"Yes. I just don't think it will work, Tucker. You in Boston, me in Rhode Island—"

"There has to be a way to make this work." He gripped her arms, his eyes pleading with her.

She took a deep breath and held it. She was about to flip the table and drop a bombshell on him. "What if I didn't go back to Plymouth U in the fall? What if I focused on researching history in the area and writing books?"

"Quit your job?"

She tilted her head to the side. "Change jobs, more accurately."

"And where would you live?"

"Well, I would probably need to travel around New England, but I could establish a home base. I hear Boston is a nice city."

"Boston is a very nice place." A wide grin spread across his face, and relief flooded Lansing's body. "And I happen to know a great condo you can live in. On the bay, close to everything, great views—"

"Handsome, sexy guy as a roommate?"

"No." He shook his head. "Not roommate. Boyfriend."

Boyfriend. It had a nice ring to it.

She inhaled deeply, held it then slowly exhaled. "You're sure this is what you want?"

His face turned serious. "I've never been more sure of anything in my life."

She leaned in and kissed him. "Well, looks like you've got yourself a committed relationship and a live-in girlfriend, Tucker Kingsley." She gave him another quick kiss and turned to walk back to the inn. "We have so much to do. I have to draft a letter of resignation, get my house on the market. Pack—ugh—another house to pack. Not looking forward to that."

Tucker chuckled beside her.

"What?" she asked.

"You sound like me a few minutes ago—lips moving a mile a minute."

Her heart was racing with excitement, and she could barely contain the happiness that flooded her. She was going to have everything she didn't know she wanted a month ago. "Sorry, just trying to think of everything I need to do."

"*Everything* will get done." He stopped in the middle of the trail. "There's only one thing we need to do right now, and that's celebrate our new living arrangement." He gathered her in his arms and pulled her close to his body.

She inhaled the smell of the trees and his unique scent. This was her happy place, wrapped up in him, gazing into his eyes, and immersed in the love he had for her. "I can't think of anything I would rather do than *celebrate* with you."

"Me, either." He pressed his lips against hers and kissed her hard.

Tingles spread across her skin and heat hit low in her belly. Every thought other than her and Tucker making love evaporated from her mind. They continued the walk back to the inn, but picked up the pace.

"Tucker, wait," Lansing said as they entered the garden. There was still something that needed to be said before they went any farther. Something she had been neglecting to tell him. Something she had never said to another man.

"Yeah?"

"I love you, too."

OTHER BOOKS IN THE SERIES

Get the Trilogy today.

Awakening, Book One by Deanndra Hall
Retribution, Book Two by Anne L. Parks
Banishing, Book Three by Jax Jillian

GET A FREE NOVELLA FROM ANNE

If you enjoyed Retribution, please consider signing up for my Newsletter and receiving my Novella, Fly Boy FREE!

CLICK HERE TO GET FLY BOY

ABOUT THE AUTHOR

Born and raised in the Rocky Mountains, Anne L. Parks has spent the last 25 years moving all over the United States. Married to the Navy – well a Commander in the Navy – Parks has lived in various locales throughout the United States. She currently resides in the Washington D.C area, and is loving every minute. When not writing, she spends her time reading, doing yoga, mountain biking, and keeping track of four kids. And drinking wine.

2013 marked her debut in publishing, with her first novel, *Strangers*, which released on her 45th birthday. Readers fell in love with a story about two people dealing with grief, and finding love again. Abby and Bryce are the perfect couple to introduce Parks as an up-and-coming author.

Her second novel, *The Return*, released in December 2013, and was the catalyst for the *Return To Me* series, a five-book series about second chance love. Other books in this series include, *Return To Newport*, *Lauren's Return*, *Returning Home*, and *RSVP: A Return To Me Christmas novella*.

Parks stepped out of her comfort zone, and delved into the paranormal with a group of highly talented authors. The result? *Elementals, An Urban Fantasy/Paranormal Romance Anthology*, about four sisters fighting to save the earth – and each other – from their deranged mother.

Currently, Parks is hard at work on her the highly suspenseful Tri-Stone Trilogy. *Of Demons & Stones*, the first book in the trilogy, and *Revenge: Of Demons & Stones Book Two*, are both available at all major distributors. Book three, *Vindication*, will be available March, 2017.

Find Anne At:
www.alparksauthor.com/
alparks@alparksauthor.com

ALSO BY ANNE L. PARKS

The Return Series

- The Return
- Return To Newport
- Lauren's Return
- Returning Home
- RSVP

The Tri-Stone Trilogy

- Of Demons & Stones
- Revenge
- Vindication

Silent Cove Series

- Awakening
- Retribution
- Banishing

Stand Alone's & Anthologies

- Strangers
- Celebrate - A Love Brothers Anthology (No longer available)
- Elementals (No longer available)

Lightning Source UK Ltd.
Milton Keynes UK
UKHW020706270222
399288UK00010B/301